The Witches of Pollok

Anne Downie

Capercaillie Books

First published by Capercaillie Books Limited in 2010.

Registered office 1 Rutland Court, Edinburgh

© Anne Downie. The moral rights of the author have been asserted.

Printed by CPI Bookmarque, Surrey

Set in Galliard by 3btype.com, Edinburgh

A catalogue record of this book is available from the British Library.

ISBN   978-1-906220-36-5

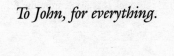

To John, for everything.

Contents

Part Three — Retribution

Epilogue

Acknowledgements

To my late brother Jim Delaney, in Canada, for his superb internet research skills and his infinite patience and persistence in ferreting out information when I drew a blank.

To Kay Strang at Capercaillie Books for her belief in me.

To my readers Kathleen Campbell, John, Mark and Susan.

To Professor Willy Maley of Glasgow University.

To Lyndsay Reilly at Capercaillie.

To the staff at Mitchell Library, Glasgow.

To the staff at Pollokshaws Library, Glasgow.

To Mark Mitchell and Professor Stephen Driscoll, Department of Archaeology, Glasgow University.

The School of History and Classics, University of Edinburgh.

The History Foundation, Virginia USA.

The Clan Maxwell Society, USA.

To Michael Boyd, Artistic Director of The Royal Shakespeare Company, who in 1990, commissioned me to write the play based on these events while he was Artistic Director of the Tron Theatre, Glasgow.

Finally and most importantly, to my husband John Downie, for living with me in the 17th Century, for his constant help, cooking and computer skills and selfless support and encouragement.

A work of fiction based on true events.

Part One

Accusation

Chapter One

The Burning

24 February 1677

Despite the occasion, a public execution, there was almost a celebratory air amongst the citizenry of Paisley. People poured from their houses, wrapped up warmly against the cold, greeting their friends and neighbours with outstretched hands. It had been one of the worst winters in memory. Snow had fallen relentlessly since the beginning of December. The roads, never great at the best of times, gouged and rutted as they were by cart-wheels, had become treacherous with ice. No horse nor human could keep his feet. The enforced hibernation had tested the patience of the townspeople. Elderly folk with no relatives to look after them, unable to venture out for food or fuel, had frozen to death in their homes.

The week before had seen the beginning of a thaw as a watery sun emerged, causing melting snow to drip from thatches. Two days of torrential rain followed, turning roads and fields into dirty grey slush, before the earth miraculously disposed of its unsightly traces and restored order once more.

The morning of the twenty-fourth of February was crisp and clear. There even seemed to be a little warmth in the bright sun. People threw open their shutters to hear the town crier announce the event for which they'd all been waiting. Five people were to be burned on Paisley Green for the bewitching of Sir George Maxwell of Pollok. The trial had gained some notoriety and all were anxious to see the accused receive retribution. Some were convinced that the same witches had been responsible for the prolonged period of foul weather. The townspeople felt they would breathe more easily when the wretched individuals were reduced to ashes. They streamed towards the Green, a heady excitement in the air, telling each other what they knew of the case. Those who had risen early to ensure the best view were now growing weary of the wait and annoyed at those, just arrived, who pushed their way to the front.

The restless murmurings amongst the crowd were suddenly silenced, replaced by macabre excitement as they watched the preparations for the executions. Sweating labourers arrived with vast quantities of faggots. Pitch was boiled up in readiness. Five people took a lot of burning. Four of them were already dead. The lifeless bodies of John Stewart, Margaret Jackson, Bessie Weir and Margery Craige were tied to their stakes; the ropes round their necks had mercifully taken their lives in return for their confessions of witchcraft. The crowds watched with interest as the prisoners' corpses were smeared with hot tar to ensure hasty incineration, the pickpockets amongst the crowd welcoming this activity. They plied their trade swiftly, avoiding the watchful eyes of the militia, there to ensure crowd control.

The trundling of a sledge being pulled over the cobbles from Paisley prison signified the event they had all been impatiently awaiting. The woman on board was barefoot. Word had got round that Jenny Mathie Stewart, the fifth to be executed for the bewitching of Sir George Maxwell of Pollok, was going to her death still proclaiming her innocence. For that reason she would be denied the right to strangulation and would be burnt alive. Preparations must have taken place at the prison for she was clothed in a light shift, her limbs already smeared with pitch. A tarred bonnet sat incongruously at a jaunty angle on top of her matted grey hair. As she drew abreast of the crowd, a hail of stones rained upon her from a group of catcalling youths, one rock striking her full in the face. It was a barely conscious figure who was helped down from the sledge. The Reverend Alexander Bell stepped forward and prayed quietly over her. The crowd jeered, angry at the idea of a witch being offered Christian consolation, but the minister's words seemed to restore Jenny Mathie. She held her head high as the executioner and his assistants hoisted her onto a tar barrel, laid against the stake, to which she was then attached with iron bands. She gazed fearlessly at the crowd, many of whom shouted abuse. Words could not hurt her. Jenny had endured so much at the torturer's hand that death itself seemed a merciful release. She said a silent prayer, glanced sadly towards the lifeless body of her son John, who was tied to the next stake and offered up both of their souls to God.

The Abbey clock struck three, the signal for the fires to be lit. Sweetmeat sellers suddenly ceased offering their wares. From experience they knew no-one had an appetite during this phase of the proceedings. As the flames took hold of each of the pyres, the smell of searing human flesh filled the nostrils, making gorges rise. The screams and struggles of Jenny Mathie as the flames from the tar barrel consumed her feet and ankles thrilled the crowd. The stone-throwing youths cheered as her shift caught fire, then disintegrated, exposing her naked flesh. As the lid of the barrel on which she was standing burned away, her body fell a few inches, but she was still visible through the flames, suspended by the iron chain binding her chest to the stake. As her charred remains roasted and sputtered in the intense heat, a cross gust of wind blew amongst the spectators who felt as if they were being suffocated by the nauseating stench. The sweetmeat sellers quickly covered their trays with muslin. A mother with a young baby pulled the blanket up and around the infant's face, hastily wiping a black mark from the child's cheek as ash flew in all directions. The tall, well dressed young woman standing at the back of the crowd had seen enough. She felt physically sick. Margaret Maxwell, daughter of Sir George Maxwell of Pollok hurried away from Paisley Green, the anguished cries of Jenny Mathie still ringing in her ears.

Chapter Two

The Letter

Three months earlier

Sir George Maxwell of Pollok was a troubled man. He gazed out at the peaceful scene below the castle window, the grass coated with an early morning frost, the fish pond glinting in the pale winter sun. Branches of the bushes below were still starched and stiff, their arthritic fingers impatiently awaiting the healing rays. Scotland seemed to have plunged into winter too quickly. A few golden leaves were hanging on tenaciously to the beech trees. He smiled. As a child, Margaret had loved to paint this view, sitting by him as he worked at his desk, tongue protruding from between her lips in childish concentration. Solid brown trunks emerged, giants, out of all proportion, daubed with golden balls of colour; the pond always blue in Margaret's youthful vision. He turned his thoughts, reluctantly, away from that happy memory and back to the letter. He read it again, frowning, thought for a moment, then crossed to the bell pull, giving it a vigorous tug. After a few moments, James Dunlop appeared. Although dressed appropriately in the livery of a servant, it was difficult to define the nature of James's particular function in the Maxwell household. Old retainer seemed inadequate to cover the myriad of roles he fulfilled under the castle roof.

'James, would you ask Mistress Margaret to come here?'

Sir George was gazing out of the window, watching the gardener busily tying up plants and clearing away dead twigs, as his daughter entered the room. As he turned, Margaret saw the troubled expression on her father's face. She hurried over to him immediately, touching his arm, concerned.

'Are you well, Father? Your pains havena' returnit?'

'No, I'm fine lass,' he hesitated for a moment, 'but it is about that period I wish to question you.' He picked up the letter from his desk.

'I've just receivit this from the Reverend Alexander Bell. He's the minister from Jenny Mathie Stewart's kirk. Sit down, lass. Let me read you it.'

Margaret seated herself near the window, as her father cleared his throat.

Dear Sir George,

I was delightit to hear of your recovery.

Sir, I beg for your intercession on behalf of a member of my flock, namely, Jenny Mathie Stewart. My reason for writing is as follows.

I have been approachit by Mary Robertson, daughter of Jenny Stewart, regarding her mother who is currently incarceratit in Paisley prison awaiting trial for witchcraft. To be precise, Mistress Stewart is accusit of bewitching your good self.

I hope the fact that you have recoverit, by the Lord's good grace, from the illness which struck you down, will allow you to examine the facts of this case and, if you, like me, harbour some doubts over the matter, you will find it in your heart to intervene.

I know little of Janet Douglas, no one seems to, except that it is purely on her testimony that this good woman has been imprisonit. I am well aquaintit, however, with the character and nature of Jenny Mathie, a God fearing woman who would no more consort with Satan than I would.

I understand that the aforesaid Janet Douglas is currently in your employ. I beg you to question this woman further. Mary Robertson and the Stewart family are convincit she is the one to blame and the one who has fabricatit a pack of lies in order to have their mother arrestit. As to Janet Douglas's reason, apart from a motiveless malignity, I cannot begin to fathom.

I trust, as a God-fearing man yourself, you will be as anxious as I am to arrive at the truth and ensure that an innocent woman is not burnit at the stake. I am sure you would not wish that on your conscience any more than I would and beg you to look into this matter further.

Your humble servant etc.'

Sir George folded the letter and looked up gravely.

'What do we know of this lass Janet Douglas? Really know?'

'Only that she has been your saviour, Father.'

'So you say and have been saying since you beggit me to take her into my employ, but do we know anything about her?'

'Only that your doctor had pronounced you as having no hope of recovery till she appearit and pointit the finger at those who bewitchit you.'

Sir George scratched his chin impatiently.

'Doctors are wise men, but they dinna ken everything. My recovery may have been entirely natural. Your feeling of obligation to Janet Douglas might be entirely misplacit.'

'If you had seen what I have of Janet Douglas's powers,' the young girl blurted out, 'you would have no doubt that she has been instrumental in saving your life.'

'Indeed,' Sir George's tone was thoughtful, probing, 'but then you never did tell me how my 'saviour' and yourself became aquaintit. When I askit you before, you changed the subject. Before any injustice is committed, it is important that I am aquaintit with all the facts, Margaret. How and where did you meet Janet Douglas?'

Margaret looked uneasy. She knew her father would not approve of what she had done that day. He sensed her hesitation and crossed over to her, putting his arm around her shoulders.

'I need to know everything. Start at the beginning. Leave nothing out.'

Chapter Three

The Glasgow Fair

Margaret had absolutely refused to accompany her father on a three day trip to her sister Marian's home in Glasgow. He had thought the pleasures of the growing town would please her and was surprised at her refusal. Situated about three and a half miles from their castle, Glasgow was a rising burgh with a rapidly expanding economy. It had overtaken Dundee and Aberdeen to become the second most important town in Scotland. Plans for a new port were already underway to accommodate the import of sugar and tobacco, in which trades its merchants were making their considerable fortunes.

All this was of little interest to Margaret. At seventeen

years of age, she craved excitement. Lengthy dinners with the town worthies at her sister's home were anathema to her. Endless discussions of plans for the new soapery, or the rise in tallow prices, or the need for the importation of whale oil with which her father and Marian's husband, James, were financially involved, bored her. She suffered from the restlessness of youth, a feeling that life was happening elsewhere. Besides, she had other plans, ones that she did not confide to her father. She knew he would refuse his permission.

The young girl felt justified in her secrecy, her defiance even, in retaliation for the way she had been treated, being excluded from a family trip to London. Her mother, sister Annabelle and little brother Zacharias were visiting Annabelle's betrothed in the English capital and would be gone for some months. Margaret raged and sulked when she found out she was to be left behind. Lady Maxwell explained gently that being in charge of the household, in their absence, would be excellent experience. Both she and Sir George envisaged a suitable, ideally advantageous, marriage for their striking looking youngest daughter, providing her restless spirit could be curbed. Margaret was intelligent, with a quick incisive mind. She vociferously objected when her brothers were sent off to school, then University, while she had to settle for the basic elements of education, the crumbs passed on by the family tutor to the female members of the family, almost as an afterthought. English and arithmetic were deemed sufficient for those whose job in life would be running a household and supervising accounts. Margaret wanted more out of life. Fortunately she had a brain which absorbed information quickly. She borrowed her brothers' books, taught herself French and Latin and devoured the contents of her father's library.

She had risen on the morning in question, resolved to make full use of her last day of freedom. Her father was due to return that night. She dressed carefully, but not showily, selecting her plainest dress and sturdiest shoes. She was anxious not to draw attention to herself; not where she was going. She felt a little nervous at the prospect, but told herself that she would not be on her own. She rang for James Dunlop and arranged to have Laurence bring the carriage round.

'Is it Paisley we're headit for, Mistress?'

'No, Laurence, Glasgow. I wish to visit the Glasgow Fair.'

James and Laurence exchanged a look, before James ventured to speak.

'Beggin' your pardon, Mistress, but I dinna think Sir George would want you to go there. It is a dangerous place.'

''Tis a good thing he's not here then,' she carried on before James tried to talk her out of it. 'Anyway, it is perfectly safe now. The stall keepers have to take turns at bearing arms and keeping the peace.'

She climbed into the carriage quickly, closing the door on further protest.

The Fair was in that part of Glasgow known as The

Butts. All her life Margaret had heard tantalising snippets of gossip about what went on there. Servants often forgot young ears and minds were like sponges, absorbing all that they overheard and trying to make sense of it. She had read about it in her father's library. There had been a fair in Glasgow ever since its great Cathedral had been built, more than five hundred years before. The citizenry of the town would meet up in the churchyard on the day of its dedication, but it had long since lost any sense of a religious occasion and now gave full rein to its secular purpose, the latter being the part that interested Margaret. She remembered, as a child, when Robbie Gillespie, one of the estate carters and a father of five little children, received a fractured skull at one of the riots there. He was never the brightest of men, but the blow seemed to have put paid to whatever intelligence he had. He never worked again and despite initial help from Sir George, the family ended up in the workhouse. Her father's subsequent appeals to the magistrates of the city and deacons of the crafts to vastly increase the fine of stallholders who did not take their turn in bearing arms, in order to keep the peace, had borne fruit.

All of this fuelled Margaret's imagination as the carriage sped along on its journey to Glasgow. She was in a reverie, gazing out at rolling fields and lush orchards whose promise of a rich harvest was already in evidence. As they galloped along a country lane bordered by wild briar rose bushes, their petals blowing in the wind and their fragrance filling her nostrils, the carriage drew to a sudden halt, almost throwing her to the ground. She looked out in alarm. Two men with leather pouches round their waists were holding up their hands in an officious manner.

'Beggin' your pardon, Mistress, they've movit these tolls further and further oot. This one took me by surprise.' Laurence held the horses firmly as he flipped a coin to the Toll Master, whose companion marked the shoes of both Laurence and James to show they had paid their dues. With a shake of the reins they were off again. Soon Margaret heard a cacophony of bagpipe music, drums and flutes mixed with the shouts and roars of an excited crowd. She looked out of the window. Ahead she could see tents and stalls with bright coloured bunting blowing in the stiff summer breeze. The carriage drew up at an inn just before The Butts, where James and Laurence tethered the horses and paid the stable boy to keep a watchful eye on the carriage.

'You canna be too careful roon these parts.' James was clearly disapproving of the whole enterprise, but knew that once his young mistress had made up her mind, nothing would stop her.

'Ca' canny, Miss Margaret! You'll ruin your shoes!' Laurence warned as he helped her down from the carriage, avoiding the muddy pothole almost directly in her path.

'Dinna leave oor side noo Mistress. This is nae place for a lady!' James admonished. He had known Margaret since she was a baby and tended to be overprotective.

'Oh, for goodness sake, wheesht! You are like twa

cluckin' hens!' Margaret rebuked impatiently. She was mes-
merised by everything around her. Two bare-chested men,
sweat glistening on their entwined bodies, were wrestling,
sinews straining, while the crowd shouted encouragement.
A stilt walker in tartan trews pretended to wobble precar-
iously, swaying dangerously towards her. James pulled her
swiftly out of the man's path before the latter 'righted'
himself, doffing his hat in cheery salute. A buxom sweetmeat seller stopped in front of Margaret, mouth-watering
slices of gingerbread, mounds of treacle candy and crum-
bly honey biscuits, laid out temptingly on the tray around
her neck.

'What wid you like, lady? It's a' delicious. Made by my
own haun.'

'Dinna touch them, Mistress.' James tried to pull
Margaret away. 'You could catch somethin'.' He attempted
to say the last part under his breath, but the woman heard
him and shouted after him, angrily. 'Ask anyone, Mary
Robertson keeps the cleanest hoose in the hale of Glasgow.
You'll catch nothin' fae me!'

Margaret's attention was already diverted by a roll of
drums coming from beyond the row of booths in front of
her. She rushed off, following the sound, the two servants
in pursuit.

'Come back, Miss Margaret,' James panted. 'If onything
happint to ye, I'd be held responsible.'

'You're relievit of all responsibility, James. It was me
forcit you to come here,' the girl said airily, as she waited

in front of a brightly coloured booth, in eager anticipation.

'Bide close by oor side. This place is hoachin' wi' thieves
and drunks.'

'Makes a change fae nippit auld ministers of the kirk
and lang windit gentlemen of the law. Father's ears will
hae drappit aff fae sheer boredom,' she laughed.

'Your sister does her best to entertain ye, Mistress.'
James's tone was reproving. 'I dinna ken why you refuse
her invitations. It is no' often she has the chance to show
ye off to Glasgow society.'

'If that's Glasgow society, then Polloktoun should hae
Royal aspirations!' Margaret answered sarcastically. Her
attention was caught as a pedlar approached, his tray a riot
of colour.

'Ribbons for the fine lady.' The man smiled, displaying
a set of black, rotting teeth. Laurence pushed him aside
roughly.

'Mind your manners, Laurence!' Margaret admonished.
'I would like the blue yin.' She handed the pedlar a coin.

'Guid health tae wear it Mistress.' The pedlar was interrupted by a second roll of drums as the drummer appeared
in front of a curtained rostrum.

'If you want your future foretellit and your past to be
revealit,' he announced, 'then gather roon yin an aw.'

'Come on.' Margaret moved nearer. 'I want to hear this!'

A curious crowd had gathered. The drummer gave
another roll on the drums and, with a great theatrical

flourish, a tall man suddenly appeared from behind the curtains. He was dressed in a flashy blue and gold showman's coat. Alan Geddes had a brash confidence about him, acquired over many years spent living on his wits, but it was coupled with an inherent seediness that no amount of fine dressing could disguise. He addressed his audience in a loud ringing tone.

'Ladies . . . and gentlemen,' he looked at the gathered throng before continuing, pointedly, 'if there be any amang ye.'

The crowd jeered at his insinuation.

'Bliddy cheek!' said Laurence. 'Beggin' your pardon, Mistress!'

Margaret waved her hand impatiently to quieten Laurence as Geddes continued.

'Freens . . . ahint this curtain is someone who will amaze and astound ye. In aw ma years comin to the great Fair o' Glasgow I hae showit ye mony wonders . . .'

'Aye, like your three heidit coo!' a burly man shouted out.

'An' your beardit bairnies!' his wife heckled.

Geddes raised his hand for silence. 'Ladies and gentlemen . . . what you are about to witness, defies any description. You are about to come face to face wi' someone whose supreme powers canny be explainit.'

'Aw it's King Cherlie!' another wag interrupted.

The crowd laughed and jeered, but were quickly silenced by another drum roll. Geddes held his hands up for attention. With a dramatic flourish, he indicated the curtained area.

'Freens . . . I give you the yin . . . the only . . . Janet Douglas!'

It may have been the drums, but it seemed like a distant rumble of thunder, causing her to shiver suddenly, Margaret remembered, as she related these events to her father. This was the first time she had come face to face with the strange young woman, whom she considered to be her father's saviour. Janet Douglas would alter their lives irrevocably and those of Jenny Mathie and the other, soon to be accused, estate workers who were to curse her nightly for their incarceration in Paisley gaol.

The girl who stepped through the curtains had a composure about her that seemed unnatural in one so young. Her age was difficult to pinpoint. She stood there quietly, seeming distanced from her surroundings. The burly heckler spoke up again.

'She hasnae got twa heids. Hey lassie! Whit's sae special aboot you?'

Geddes intervened smoothly. 'Sir, she canny answer ye. The Lord in His wisdom has made her a dumbie . . . wi' nae power o' verbal communication.'

There was a sympathetic murmuring from the crowd, but Geddes quietened them. 'Save your sympathy, freens . . . Janet here has nae need for pity . . . for Mother Nature has compensated twinty times ower.' There was another dramatic drum roll, before he continued.

'You see afore ye nae ordinary lass, but yin who is blessit with the most extraordinary powers.'

'Oh aye, let's see them!' another heckler had found his voice.

'A wee bit sweetie, ma'am . . . sir? It's gawn tae be a lang nicht.' Mary Robertson, the sweet-meat seller, took advantage of the heckler's interruption to pass through the crowd, much to the annoyance of Geddes, who was trying to win back control of his audience.

'Madam!' he barked. 'Wid ye kindly refrain frae hawkin' your wares while I'm aboot ma business.'

'It's a free country!' she retorted spiritedly.

'That's nae whit Cherlie says!' the burly heckler was getting into his stride, grinning round at the audience for approval.

'Anyway,' Mary continued dismissively, 'you dinna own the hale fair-grun'.'

'I'll speak tae you later, Mary Robertson!' There was a warning note in Geddes's voice.

'Oh I canna wait!' she answered. The mock sexiness in her tone drew laughter from the audience. Margaret was thoroughly enjoying the entertainment the crowd was providing. This was what she had been missing. Geddes signalled again to the drummer, whose pounding silenced the rabble once more.

'Ladies and Gentlemen!' Geddes's voice boomed out.

'I am not going to try to explain this lassie's powers. I will merely demonstrate them. I would like a volunteer to pass up any object of a personal nature . . . Janet here will then astound you by revealing information known only by its owner.' He rounded on the burly heckler. 'C'mon, you sir, who has been doin' aw the shoutin'. Hae you an object for us?'

The man grinned round at the crowd and felt in his pockets before passing up a crumpled handkerchief. Geddes held it gingerly at arms length between thumb and finger, as if fearing contamination.

'I will not deduce the obvious fae this,' he said, winking knowingly at his audience. 'I'll leave that to our expert.' He indicated Janet. 'Friends . . . prepare to witness a miracle. This lassie canna speak but she has the power tae transfer thought. I will become the instrument o' Janet's speech. Her thoughts will travel from her mind to ma mooth.'

There was a stirring of interest from the crowd. Confident that he now had their attention, he continued. 'I have promised you a miracle, ladies and gentlemen, and Alan Geddes always keeps his word . . . but I must request a perfect silence, if you please.'

Another dramatic drum roll broke the silence. Margaret craned to see what was happening. The young woman, Janet Douglas, had shut her eyes. Geddes held the handkerchief in one hand and took Janet's hand in the other. There was silence for a few moments, before he started speaking in a strangely flat, but audible tone. 'William Soutar, to whom this kerchief belongs . . .'

The burly man nudged his wife, a red faced woman, whose girth exceeded his own. She smiled, delighted at the attention. 'You are having fornicating relations with one who is not your wife,' Geddes continued.

Soutar looked startled. The smile left his wife's face instantly.

'Whit? Let's hear more!' she said, her voice a mixture of disbelief and anger.

'This adulterous relationship has continuit these twa months past,' Geddes intoned, in the same expressionless manner. Soutar was beginning to look extremely uncomfortable, his face almost willing Geddes to stop, but his accuser continued. 'You have giftit this woman many tokens o' your love. Includit in these, be siller, lace, sweetmeats an' locks o' your ain hair.'

Mrs Soutar, now apoplectic with rage, grabbed her unfortunate husband by the hair, screaming like a madwoman.

'I'll gie ye some mair hair for your hoor, ya messin! I'll tear oot your hale heid!'

Soutar wrenched himself free, painfully, leaving a few strands in her grasp, before running off, pursued by his angry wife.

'Come back ye fornicatin' swine ye!' she bellowed after him.

The crowd laughed and jeered, urging Mrs Soutar on, until pursued and pursuer disappeared from view.

Aware that he now had his audience's full attention, Geddes moved swiftly on. 'May we have another object, ladies and gentlemen? I'm offerin' you the opportunity o' a lifetime. A chance to hae your future foretellit,' he urged. 'Come on . . . dinna be feart!'

Without a moment's hesitation, Margaret reached up and removed one of the combs she used to tame her unruly curls. 'Here Laurence, give him this.'

Laurence looked wary. 'Are ye sure, Miss Margaret?'

'Best to leave these queer fowk alane.' James tried to lead her away. She pulled herself from his grip, angrily.

'Do as you're telt!' she ordered, an unusually censorious note in her voice.

Reluctantly, Laurence pushed through the crowd to the front. 'Here ma mannie.' He handed up the silver and lilac comb to Geddes. 'And mind, I want that back!'

'Widnae hae thought it wis your colour sir,' Geddes winked at the audience and was rewarded with laughter. A number of them had been frequenting the ale stalls and were in drunken good humour. He turned to the young woman beside him who had remained expressionless and composed throughout. He raised his voice, 'Are ye ready Janet?' She nodded.

He held up Margaret's comb and took Janet's hand. There was a momentary silence during which Margaret felt a frisson of excitement. Geddes started speaking in the same flat expressionless manner as before.

'Now . . . the owner of this object is a young lady of quality. She is paying a visit to our fair town of Glasgow . . . she bides near Polloktoun and . . . yes . . . is the daughter of Sir George Maxwell of Pollok.'

Margaret started in amazement. How could he possibly know this? Had Geddes seen her before? She glanced at

Laurence and James, who were looking uneasy. She looked up at Geddes, waiting for him to continue, but the colour had drained from the showman's face. He was holding his head as if in pain, the girl, Janet, mirrororing his actions. With difficulty he began to speak once more.

'She . . . oh . . . oh . . .' his voice trailed off. He writhed, as if in agony. The crowd began to mutter in alarm. Margaret pushed her way to the front, the servants trying to hold her back.

'Stay away, Miss Margaret!' There was fear in Laurence's voice but Margaret faced Geddes, steadily.

'What is it you see?' she asked. 'I want to know.'

Geddes spoke with some difficulty, his face contorting with pain.

'Your faither . . . oh . . .' He broke off, doubled over, clutching his side. The girl, Janet, was standing stock still, staring fixedly ahead in a trance like state.

'Whit aboot my father?' Margaret's tone was worried, urgent. 'Tell me!'

'He has been struckit doon! Return to the castle now! He is calling for you,' Geddes said hoarsely. 'Oh . . . I feel his pain! . . . Go . . . go hame at once before the life leaves his wrackit body!'

The colour suddenly drained from his face and he dropped to the ground, motionless. Janet continued to stare ahead, unmoved.

The crowd were silent, stunned. Margaret was suddenly afraid.

Laurence put his arm round her. 'Dinna be feart, Mistress. It's just trickery.'

'Take me home,' she urged, in a state of great agitation. 'Father is ill. He needs me.'

The crowd were whispering and muttering uneasily. No-one had approached the prostrate figure of Geddes, unsure of whether his apparent collapse was part of the act. He lay there, deathly still, for a few moments, before rising, very unsteadily, to his feet. Janet stood there as if detached from the proceedings, making no move to help him.

'Let's get the hell oota here!' James ushered Margaret quickly away.

Chapter Four

Illness

Margaret remembered little of the journey back to Pollok, she told her father. Her concern was solely for him as fear and anxiety created their own troubling scenarios in her mind. Sir George's memory of that night was also extremely hazy, lapsing, as he was, in and out of consciousness. He had felt unwell on his return home from his daughter Marian's house. After that, all he recalled was the excruciating pain from which drugged sleep was a welcome respite.

As soon as the carriage reached the castle, Margaret hurried past the stricken house-servants, already knowing what they were about to tell her and ran up the broad staircase to her father's bedroom. She tiptoed over to the bed where his physician, Doctor Bremner, hovered helplessly. Her father lay there, deathly still. Shocked by his altered appearance, she took his hand in hers, fear gripping her. Had she brought this on him? She knew he would not have approved of her visit to the Glasgow Fair. By her wilfulness, had she caused him to be struck down?

'How is he Doctor?'

Doctor Bremner put a finger to his lips before drawing her aside. He looked down at her young, anxious face. It would be easy to give false hope, but it was too late for that. She had the right to the truth.

'Not too well, Miss Margaret,' he said gravely. 'His fever is ower high.'

'I telt him no' to visit Paisley last month,' the girl said worriedly. 'They say there's still plague in that toon.'

'It is no' the plague, Mistress.'

'Then whit ails him ?'

'He complains his left side is bein' stabbit. The pain is takin' a' his strength away.'

'What can be done for him? Surely there is . . .'

'I gave him some physic, earlier,' Bremner interrupted gently, 'but to no avail.'

'Have you opened a vein?'

'I have, lass, for I feared he had pleurisy.'

Her eyes longed for reassurance, but Bremner, in all honesty, could not provide it. He felt it his duty to prepare the young girl for the worst.

'The pain has increasit and his fever continues to rise.'

'There must be something else you can do, surely?' Tears pricked the back of her eyes.

The old doctor took her hands in his. 'I hae usit aw ma skill, Miss Margaret. It is in the Lord's hands noo.'

'May I see him, alone, Doctor?'

'Aye, lass, but dinna tire him. He's in sair need o' aw his strength.'

He quietly withdrew, closing the door behind him.

Margaret crossed back to the bed. Her father lay, eyes closed, a disturbing grey pallor on his face she had never seen before.

'Father . . . can you hear me?' She put her lips close to his ear.

He slowly opened his eyes and turned his head with a great deal of effort. 'Margaret . . . is that you?' he asked weakly.

'It is Father. I'm here.'

'Thank the guid Lord.' He reached for her hand. 'I was feart I'd quit this world without takin' leave o' you.'

'Dinna talk like that.' Margaret fought back tears. 'You canna leave us.'

'You best contact your mother and the family.' He suddenly writhed in pain, the blood draining from his face.

Margaret called urgently for the doctor, who rushed in, James in tow.

Bremner took a swift look at his patient, 'Help me lift him up, James.'

The doctor put a glass to Sir George's lips. 'Take some more laudanum, Sir. 'Twill ease the pain.'

Margaret could not bear to witness her father's distress. James put his hand comfortingly on her shoulder. 'It would be best if you leave him, Miss Margaret,' he said. 'He needs rest.'

The girl did not seem to hear him. She stood there, helplessly, unable to move .

'Come on, Miss Margaret,' he repeated gently. 'Leave it to the Doctor. He kens best whit to dae.'

He led her to the door and handed her over to the care of a maidservant. Margaret drew away from the girl, fell down on her knees and started to pray. She was not particularly religious. In fact, she normally found it hard to keep her concentration on higher things at the kirk on Sunday, given as she was to examining the architecture of the church or the best bonnets of the ladies in the congregation. The Old Testament, with its tales of dragons, filial sacrifice and bears who ate children as punishment for the fairly innocuous sin of name calling, all apparently in the name of the Lord, really taxed her credulity. The divisions within Christianity itself reinforced her doubts; ministers within whose pastoral care she grew up, being forcibly removed from their parishes and livings for the sake of differences in liturgical interpretation. Riots and killings due to enforced episcopacy: the installation of bishops as chief clerics smacked of Popery to Presbyterian Scotland. That each Christian was convinced his was the correct path to salvation, made her despair. Would any God worthy of the title be happy with this divisiveness amongst his flock? The King, Charles the Second, made it known that he wanted to draw a line under these divisions, but they were still present. The past ten years of Margaret's young life had been fraught with rebellions, as adherants to the National League and Covenant, drawn up in 1638 against the attempt to impose a new liturgy and prayer book upon the Church of Scotland, fought to preserve the true Protestant reformed religion. Her father, too, had been imprisoned for his Covenanting sympathies. All this shook the very foundations of her faith. She was convinced that, if indeed there was a God, he would be totally disgusted at the intolerance rife amongst his flock. That day, however, with her father's life in jeopardy, she set all doubts aside and prayed that he might be spared with a fervour that must have surprised the Almighty Himself.

Margaret had arisen early next morning and rushed to her father's bedside. She was distraught to find there was little improvement in his condition. She sat down to write to her mother, urging her to bring the family home. Their coach journey from London would take almost two weeks. She prayed that her father would last until their return. He was always at pains to protect her mother from bad news, knowing her nervous temperament. She lifted her quill. How to stress the urgency of the situation without being too alarmist? Yet the gravity of her father's illness demanded absolute honesty. This was no time for equivocation.

She was interrupted by the servant, James Dunlop, asking her to come down to the Great Hall. A number of the estate workers had heard of the decline in Sir George's health and wished to enquire about his condition. Margaret responded, through tears, that she did not feel like facing them, but James tactfully pointed out that it was her responsibility as the only member of the family present. Chastened by his words, she made her way downstairs to meet them.

She vaguely recognised the older woman who appeared to be their spokeswoman, also the girl at her side, but she could not put a name to them immediately. James came swiftly to her rescue.

'Miss Margaret, you ken the Widow Mathie, wife o' Mr Stewart, the late under Miller o' the Shaw-mill and her dochter Annabil?'

'I do indeed. My faither spoke highly o' your late husband, Mistress Stewart. A richt good worker by all accounts.'

'Aye . . . ower guid Miss Margaret,' Jenny Mathie said dryly. 'That's why he is in the Shaws cemetery the day. I hope to God your puir faither will no' be joinin' him.'

Margaret was taken aback by the woman's bluntness but managed to keep her composure.

'Amen to that, Mistress,' she said. 'I thank you for coming here today.' She recognised the blacksmith and one of the gardeners hovering in the background. 'And you Hector and Douglas, I ken how busy you all are. My father and the family appreciate all your kind wishes and messages o' sympathy. All we can do is pray for Divine intervention on his behalf. I fear it is only his stubborn spirit that's keepit him here . . .'

She broke off as the servant, Laurence, burst into the hall clutching a letter. 'Excuse me Miss Margaret,' he said, out of breath, 'but I hae an urgent message for ye.' He handed her the note. 'It is frae her! The dumbie fae Glesca Fair.'

Margaret quickly opened it. There was a short message written in bold clear handwriting.

I must see you immediately. I can cure your father.

The letter was unsigned.

'Where did you get this?' she asked.

'She gied it me just now. Her that foretellit your father's illness.'

'She's here?'

'Aye Mistress,' said Laurence. 'She is ootside.'

'Show her in,' said Margaret without hesitation.

As Laurence hurried out, James stepped forward and spoke in a cautious whisper. 'Ca' canny. Miss Margaret. How does she ken these things?'

'I dinna understand it either, but I'll talk tae anyone who says they can help Father,' she said fervently.

Laurence returned with Janet Douglas. It was, indeed, the girl from the Fair. Margaret noticed a wary look on the faces of some of the estate workers as Laurence propelled the girl forward. Janet stopped in front of Margaret and stared into her face intently. She was breathing heavily, as if under great physical stress. Then her head began to circle slowly, while her eyelids fluttered. The others moved back, but Margaret, though afraid, stood her ground. Some of the estate workers began to mutter in alarm.

'Keep awa Mistress!' urged James. There was real fear in his voice.

'Quiet!' Margaret ordered. 'She is trying to tell me something!'

Janet was mouthing, attempting to speak. With a great effort, she managed to produce a high pitched note, one that seemed more animal than human. She seized Margaret's wrists, looking into her eyes earnestly, trying desperately to communicate. Some of the workers covered their ears, in an attempt to blot out the terrifying sound. It suddenly stopped. Janet said one word loudly and clearly. There was no mistaking the word which came from her lips.

'Witchcraft!'

The others looked at one another in fear and alarm.

'What are you saying?' Margaret asked her in disbelief. 'Someone has bewitchit my father?'

Janet nodded vigorously.

'Do you ken who?'

Janet nodded again.

'Tell me . . . in God's name,' Margaret pleaded, 'who has causit his pain?'

James found his courage and stood by his mistress's side. 'Give us a name,' he demanded. 'We need a name.'

Once again Janet uttered the animal sound but at an even higher pitch. The others fell back in fear as she spun round. She stopped suddenly in her tracks with her arm outstretched, her finger pointing straight at Jenny Mathie.

'Jenny Mathie Stewart,' said James. 'Is she the one?'

Janet nodded vigorously.

'Whit's goin' on?' the older woman asked, confused. 'Whit's she sayin'?'

'That you are a witch, Jenny Mathie,' said James accusingly.

'She's haverin'!' Jenny said indignantly. 'The lassie's mad! She disnae ken whit she's speakin' aboot.'

'Whit have you done to Sir George?' asked Laurence threateningly.

'Me?' Jenny was astounded. 'Nothin' . . . I've nothin' agin the laird. He's aye been guid to me. I'd never wish him ill.'

'That's nae whit I've heard!' Hector, the blacksmith, suddenly found his voice.

'What have you heard? Speak up mannie!' Margaret demanded.

'She cursit the laird because he threatened that son o' hers.' The man looked round at the others for confirmation. A number of them nodded in agreement.

'Who is her son?' Margaret asked.

'John Stewart,' said Hector, now enjoying being centre of attention.

'That rogue!' James's tone was contemptuous.

'Whit's this all aboot James? Is there any truth in it?' Margaret was mystified. 'Did my father threaten her son?'

'Nae withoot cause Miss Margaret,' James explained.

'That rascal brokit into Sir George's orchards and strippit near every tree till it wis sterk nakit.'

'Aye an' then wis brass neckit enough tae sell the laird's apples fae a cairt in the Shaws,' Laurence added indignantly.

'An' did faither hae him punishit or what?'

'The fly young tyke took wing, Mistress' James replied. 'Flew awa to the Darnley last I heard. Sir George only threatened him wi' the micht o' the law if he returnit.'

'An' he was quite within his richts to dae so,' Laurence added.

Margaret turned to Jenny angrily. 'And was this reason to bewitch him?'

Jenny was now agitated, 'I tell you the dumbie's lying.' Her daughter Annabil looked terrified at the way the questioning was going. 'I widnae ken how tae bewitch even if I wantit to!' her mother said.

'And did you want to Jenny Mathie?' James's tone was accusatory. 'You were angry at the laird for threatenin' your son, were you no'?'

'I was upset that I didnae see oor John for nigh on a year,' Jenny answered, 'but I never harmit Sir George. I swear it!'

James turned to Annabil. 'And whit do you ken aboot this business?'

'Keep ma dochter oot o this,' Jenny said fiercely. 'She's but a bairn. She kens nae mair than me.'

'She's got a guid Scots tongue in her heid,' Laurence answered, equally sharply. 'Let her yase it.'

James put a restraining hand on Laurence's arm. He knew Annabil, a shy little creature, young for her fourteen years. A late, unexpected infant, arriving when Jenny Mathie was in middle age, thinking herself past the age of child bearing. As a consequence, she was treated as the baby of the family, fiercely protected by her mother.

'Annabil . . . whit can ye tell us, lass?' he asked gently.

'I ken nothin' . . . honest, Maister.' The colour had drained from the young girl's face. She was clearly terrified.

She backed away as Janet Douglas approached, once again making the high pitched noise. Janet's outstretched arm pointed clearly at Annabil, accusingly. Again there was no mistaking the word she uttered, one that struck cold fear in the hearts of all who heard it. 'Witchcraft!'

Maternal fury overcame fear, however, as Jenny Mathie Stewart grabbed Janet by the hair. 'You lyin' bitch!'

Laurence and James moved quickly to restrain Jenny as Annabil fell to the floor weeping. The crowd were muttering amongst themselves, fearfully. Margaret, remembering her position, took command.

'These are serious charges, Janet Douglas,' she said. 'You cannot make accusations withoot proof.'

The crowd watched closely as Janet Douglas took a piece of paper from her pocket and handed it to Margaret. It appeared to be a drawing, of what Margaret was unsure. She handed it to the servant.

'Can ye mak anything o' this James?'

James studied it for a moment, his lips pursed. 'Looks

like the plan o' a hoose.' He pointed at the paper. 'See, the fire-place is weel markit.'

'Whose house is this?' asked Margaret.

Janet pointed to Jenny Mathie, then back to the paper. She made an urgent movement towards the door.

'She's telling us to go there,' said Laurence, almost under his breath. He was feeling a little out of his depth.

'Whit's there? Will we find proof o' witches work?' James asked.

Janet Douglas took the paper from Margaret and turned it over.

On the other side was a crude drawing of a doll.

'Look Mistress!' said Laurence. 'It has pins in its side!'

Fear gnawed at Margaret. 'Oh, my God! Is that what has happint to Father?'

Janet nodded. The whisperings amongst the estate workers grew louder, accusatory. Annabil clutched her mother's hand in absolute terror at the wave of antagonism now engulfing them.

'It is a lie! I ken nothin aboot this!' Jenny Mathie shouted angrily.

Her denial seemed to spur Janet Douglas to further feverish activity. She grabbed Laurence and James by the hands. They were surprised at her strength as she tried to pull them towards the door.

'Do as she wishes,' Margaret commanded. 'Go with her to Jenny Mathie's house. Find out the truth o' the matter.'

'I dinna like meddlin' in these things,' James said

uneasily. We should report this to the Kirk or the Privy Cooncil.'

'Father will die if we dinna tak action richt noo, James.' Margaret's tone was desperate, pleading.

'I winna hae that on ma conscience,' the older man said. 'Richt Laurence, we'll go straicht away.' He turned to Janet Douglas. 'You come wi' us, if you please.'

Jenny Mathie was at the door ahead of them. 'You can aw come,' she said defiantly. 'I hae nothin' to hide. You'll find oot for yirsels who is the liar here.'

Margaret was about to follow them but heard a cry of pain coming from the room above. She bounded up the stairs two at a time.

'Father, hold on. I'm coming!

* * *

Whether it was his daughter's prayers that had been responsible for his recovery, or the later intervention of Janet Douglas, Sir George was not yet sure. They had indeed found waxen images, pierced by pins, hidden in Jenny Mathie Stewart's house, just as the young girl had indicated. Despite her protestations of innocence, Jenny Mathie had been arrested and was now in Paisley gaol awaiting trial.

Sir George was seriously pondering the sequence of events, so much so that he forgot to rebuke Margaret for her trip to Glasgow Fair, a trip he would most certainly have forbidden. How to proceed? The Reverend Bell's letter was very much on his mind. The man was right. Jenny Mathie Stewart would almost certainly die at the stake. Thomas Ramsay, the self styled 'Commissioner for Witchcraft', had a questionable reputation. Once arrested and interrogated by him, few were spared the flames. Sir George did not want the death of Jenny Mathie Stewart on his conscience if she was indeed innocent. He needed to investigate further and with haste. Margaret, too, determined to make her own enquiries.

Chapter Five

Torture

Jenny Mathie Stewart had been, at least temporarily, silenced. She lay, feet clamped in heavy irons, half naked and unconscious on the stinking straw which covered the floor of the damp, freezing, foetid dungeon in Paisley prison; her home for the past four weeks. Blood streaked gouges from two dozen lashes were now congealing on her back. No matter the punishments inflicted upon her, and there had been many, the outcome was always the same. At the end of each brutal session, though half-dead, either from enduring sleep deprivation, thumbscrew torture or being whipped in the prison yard with such ferocity that the flesh was flayed from her back, the first words from her mouth were always the same.

'I'm no' a witch. I am innocent!'

This constant denial was severely testing the patience of Thomas Ramsay. He had, mistakenly, thought that Jonet Mathie, known to friends and family as Jenny, arrested for the alleged bewitching of Sir George Maxwell of Pollok, in the year of Our Lord 1676, would be easy to break. He had assumed, at sixty years of age, Mathie would be only too willing to confess. In his experience, the infirmities of old age, coupled with the harrowing conditions in the plague-ridden, rat-infested cells of Paisley prison would be enough to weaken her endurance. Jenny suffered from rheumatism so severe that on winter mornings, when the cold rendered her bones stiff and sore, she struggled to rise from her warm bed. Now, in a freezing cell, with her legs crossed and tied in such a way that all the weight of her body rested deliberately on her arthritic hips, the pain was excruciating. It felt as if the very blood in her veins was trapped. She had lost count of the number of days in which she had endured this agony. Ramsay also ensured she was denied food or sleep, which led to her increasing confusion. At the end of these sessions, prisoners normally confessed to whatever allegation he cared to throw at them and, most importantly, gave the names of others involved, saving him time and money. Jenny Mathie, however, was an exception.

Money was a prime motivator for Ramsay. As an itinerant

professional witch-pricker, responsible for locating the so-called devil's mark on the body of the accused, the more witches he brought to trial, the more his reputation and income grew. He had just been offered thirty pounds Scots for a trip to St Andrews, where two old women were suspected of bewitching cattle. Ramsay was, therefore, anxious to bring the case of the Pollok witch to a swift conclusion. That he was thwarted in his intentions by this stubborn old woman angered him. Whenever she could muster the energy, she shouted her innocence. Ramsay had never countenanced such resistance. He was determined to break it.

He was, of course, unaware of the source of Jenny's strength. A number of grateful women in Polloktoun might have enlightened him. Many had called on Jenny's services as midwife. She had delivered scores of babies over the years. Whenever mothers-to-be were in the severe pains of childbirth she would offer the same advice. 'Imagine you're no' here. Think o' some happy thought. Of the bairn you'll be nursing efter this is ower.'

This mind controlling technique had always worked for her. She'd tried it with her first born Mary, now married and living in Glasgow, on Annabil, her youngest and with her only son, John. Perhaps it would not have been such a happy thought if Jenny had known the trouble the boy would cause her over the years. He had always been unruly, but he had a good heart and had promised to take care of Annabil while their mother was in gaol. She had told him not to bring the young girl to see her in prison.

Annabil was terrified that she, too, might be incriminated, remembering that Janet Douglas's accusation was also against her. Jenny wished to spare her sensitive and highly strung young daughter any more suffering.

Chapter Six

The Dinner Party

Margaret found it difficult to conceal her irritation. Seated at dinner beside Gilbert Pettigrew, a young probate lawyer making a name for himself in Scottish circles, was taxing her patience. It was apparent that her father had invited him as a potential suitor. Her parents had dropped his name casually into the conversation and sung his praises too many times to be coincidental. He was tolerable looking, she admitted, but unattractively and totally self-obsessed. Margaret always considered the art of conversation to be a two way process. Not apparently in Pettigrew's book. She asked him a number of polite questions about the law and was treated to a monologue broken only by his noisy mastication of the veal, chicken and fried trout put in front of him. Not once did he ask her a question about herself. She found this a common trait amongst the young men she had been introduced to recently. Why was this? Did they consider women to be mere decoration, incapable of expressing an opinion?

The real source of her irritation was due largely to the fact that she was seated the whole length of a vast oak table away from Sir George Sinclair, Professor of Philosophy at Glasgow University. She knew that her father's main purpose in inviting the professor was to have him question Janet Douglas. That she was to be excluded from the interview with the girl seemed most unfair. After all, she was the one who had first come across Janet at the Glasgow Fair. It was she who was present in the Great Hall of Pollok dealing with the estate workers the morning after Sir George had been struck down. She was witness to the entrance of Janet Douglas who, miraculously, seemed to have recovered her speech sufficiently to accuse Jenny Mathie and her daughter of witchcraft. Her father's stated reason for excluding her from the interview with Janet Douglas was that he was wary of putting the girl on guard. He had no wish to make Janet feel she was the one on trial. Some gentle enquiries from Professor Sinclair would, he hoped, elicit the answers they sought.

Sinclair was intrigued. The letter he had received from Sir George Maxwell inviting himself and his wife to dinner at the castle had contained an interesting postscript.

I have someone I wish you to meet who puzzles me greatly. Perhaps you might provide me with some insight.

Sir George was a generous benefactor to the University, but that was not the only reason for the Professor's acceptance. He considered the man a friend. He knew of his recent troubles and was anxious to be of help. As the carriage drove under the archway and through the woods, he had caught sight of the castle, a fortified tower house and felt a strange sense of unease. A thoughtful, scholarly man, not given to flights of fancy, he was at pains to hide his feelings of foreboding from his host.

They had dined exquisitely. Sir George always kept an excellent table. The wood panelled room hung with tapestries and large gilt framed family portraits, lit by flattering candlelight from half a dozen pairs of silver candlesticks, looked magnificent. Their host had made only a brief reference to Janet Douglas until now. The arrest of Jenny Mathie Stewart on his estate was now common knowledge.

When the formal meal was over, the fruit and confectionery eaten and the wine quaffed, Sir George sent Margaret, acting as hostess in her mother's absence, along with the other guests, Doctor Bremner, Gilbert Pettigrew and the Professor's wife, to the Long Gallery to view his latest purchase, four paintings from the Dutch School. Margaret tried to hide her annoyance both at her exclusion from the interview and the unwelcome attentions of Gilbert Pettigrew.

Her own attempts to strike up a conversation with Janet Douglas had met with little success. The girl always seemed to be backing away. Margaret expected some spirit of friendliness from her. After all, Margaret was the one who suggested she be given employment and a roof over her head at the castle when the girl asked for a position in the household, following the arrest of Jenny Mathie. Janet had explained that Alan Geddes, the showman, had beaten her for frightening his customers away after her revelations about Sir George's illness.

She had lost her job and was destitute. Margaret persuaded her father to give her the position of under housemaid, but there was no indication of gratitude or any recognisable emotion from Janet Douglas. Perhaps Professor Sinclair would have more success in breaking down the barrier she seemed to have built around herself.

Sir George led the Professor to the library where he rang the bell for Laurence.

'Ask Janet Douglas to join us.'

He turned to Sinclair, a troubled look in his eyes. 'I am most grateful for your visit. This wretchit business has wrackit my mind as weel as my body.'

'I gatherit from what you said earlier that you were troubled. Tell me what ails you,' the Professor said 'what you really think o' this affair.'

'I dinna ken what to think . . . I feel somewhat responsible,' Sir George replied.

'Now ye are not tellin' me, Sir George, that a man who has come as far as you have in society suffers yet fae oor national affliction?'

'To which particular affliction do you refer, Professor? We hae so many.'

'Yin of self-doubt.' The Professor gave a hint of a smile. 'The habit o' beating oorsels on the breist in moments o' crisis, or when things seem beyond oor ken.'

'Aye . . . weel I fear I must plead guilty to that charge,' Sir George said ruefully, 'but then I find the disposition of those who flail awa at folk unable to defend themselves even mair reprehensible. Seems to me those pernicious wretches tend to find their targets in the weakest and most vulnerable breists.'

'But that tendency is, regrettably, a universal one,' the Professor said.

'Maybe so, but roon here we hae an unnatural appetite for it.'

'Sir George, have you considert that those self-same appetites may look for satisfaction in unusual places?'

'I'm not sure I understand you, Professor.'

Sinclair looked serious. 'I am suggesting that there are those amang us who find the canons of law and church do nothing but keep them in their place. If that place is not pleasing to them then they might be inclinit to invoke other help and . . . ' he shrugged, 'to Hell with the consequence.'

'You mean the help of Satan? You think that there may be truth in Janet Douglas's story? That the widow Stewart and perhaps even her daughter practised his evil rites.'

'Anything is possible, Sir George. I merely suggest we keep our minds open to any circumstance.'

Sir George looked troubled. 'Of course,' he said quietly.

'You have told Janet Douglas of my visit?' the Professor enquired.

'No,' Sir George answered. 'I thought it best to catch her unpreparit.'

The Professor pursed his lips. 'You think she is a scheming lass, then?'

'No,' Sir George answered hastily. 'I honestly dinna ken what to make of her. I've not encounterit her like afore. You see she . . .'

He saw a warning look cross Sinclair's face and turned round quickly. Janet Douglas was standing inside the door. He wasn't sure when she had appeared. She seemed to have glided silently into the room. He crossed to her hastily.

'Oh . . . I didna hear you come in, lass. Janet, this is Professor Sinclair of Glasgow University. He is Professor of Philosophy there. He wants very much to meet you.'

Sinclair held out his hand. 'I am delightit to make your acquaintance, Janet. I've heard a great deal about you.'

She said nothing but looked at him inscrutably. There was no warmth in her look, he noticed, but composure beyond her years.

Sinclair indicated a seat, but she remained standing.

He crossed nearer to her and addressed her in a friendly tone. 'Sir George has telt you the nature o' my subject. Do you know what Philosophy is, Janet?'

'The seeking after wisdom or knowledge, sir,' she said. 'In particular, that which deals with ultimate reality.'

Sinclair and Sir George exchanged surprised looks. 'Correct, Janet.' Sinclair said smoothly. 'I seek knowledge. I wish to know more about you, my dear. Sir George has telt me something of your powers. I would like to ask you some questions about yourself. Have you no objection?'

For the first time she looked uncomfortable. 'I do not like answering questions, sir,' she said. 'It pains me.'

Sinclair took a silver coin from his pocket and handed it to her.

'I have found silver to have pain reducing qualities,' he smiled. 'What say you?'

'I will answer where I can, sir,' she said, pocketing the coin.

'Good.' Sinclair looked at her questioningly. 'I understand that when Sir George's daughter, Margaret, met you at the Glasgow Fair you appeared to have lost the power of speech. Was this a fairground trick or a genuine affliction?'

'It was no trick sir,' she said, a hint of annoyance. 'I was without speech.'

'For how long had you suffered this loss?'

'For as long as I can remember.'

'Yet you speak as one practised in language,' Sinclair said curiously. 'How do you account for that?'

'I cannot, sir,' she answered smoothly.

'Can you account for your recovery?' asked the Professor.

'It was the embrocation.'

'Embrocation?' Sir George asked, surprised. This was news to him. Janet turned towards him.

64

'Yes, Sir George . . . Album Graecum. I applied it every night as revealit.'

Sir George and the Professor exchanged another look.

'Revealit?' The Professor was anxious to hear more.

'In my vision sir. I was told to apply it every night around the throat.'

'Have you any of this miraculous mixture left?' Sinclair asked curiously.

'No sir. I was using the last of it when my speech returnit.'

'I see'. Sinclair tried to hide his scepticism. 'And the container?'

'Thrown away,' the girl said unabashed. 'I had no further use of it.'

Professor Sinclair glanced at the library shelf and extracted two books. He handed one, an English translation of Sophocles' *Electra,* to Janet.

'Would you open that book and read from it,' he instructed. 'Any page you like.' Janet opened it and without the slightest hesitation read in a clear voice.

'Brother in Heaven's name
Let him not speak a word or plead his cause.
When a poor wretch is in the toils of fate
What can a brief reprieve avail him? No slay him
outright and having slain him give his corpse
to such grave makers as is meet,
Far from our sight.'

The Professor pressed further. 'You are familiar with the writing of Sophocles?' he asked.

'No, sir,' replied Janet.

'You read very fluently.' Sinclair handed the other book, a copy of Euripides' *The Bacchae* in its original Greek. 'Try this one if you will.'

She opened it at the last page and again read without hesitation.

> *'There be many shapes of mystery*
> *And many things God makes to be,*
> *Past hopes or fear.*
> *And the end men looketh for cometh not,*
> *And a path is there where no man thought*
> *So hath it fallen here.'*

'Why did you choose that particular passage from Euripides?' the Professor asked, curiously.

Janet shrugged. 'Because I liked it.'

'Are you aware that you were translating it from Greek?' asked Sinclair.

'No, sir.'

'Where did you learn to speak Greek?' Sir George asked, astonished.

'I do not know sir.'

'Come, come lass. You must ken where you were schoolit!' There was more than a hint of frustration in Sir George's voice. Was this girl playing games with them? Professor Sinclair held up a restraining hand.

'Sit down, lass. Perhaps you would care for a glass of something? I am sure Sir George has no objection.'

The girl sat down on a heavy oak chair. 'I want nothing sir. Thank you.'

'Janet Douglas . . . that is your given name?' Sinclair asked.

'It was the name I was called by all who knew me.'

'Who are your parents?'

'I do not remember, sir.'

Sir George again interrupted impatiently. 'Someone must have brought you up.'

For the first time, the girl looked a little upset. 'Yes,' she almost whispered.

'Who was it, Janet?' the Professor asked gently. His tone was solicitous, but the girl remained silent. After a few moments he crossed over and stood near her chair, using the same gentle tone.

'Janet, why not tell me? You have nothing to fear.'

When she eventually spoke, her voice was low, hesitant. Sir George had to strain in order to hear her. 'I was kept when I was very young by a poor woman.'

'Was she a relative?' Sinclair enquired.

'No sir.'

'How did you come to be there?'

'I do not know sir.'

Frustrated by this lack of progress, Sir George intervened again. 'Is this woman still alive?'

The girl shrugged, 'She may be sir.'

'You do not keep in touch with the woman who brought you up?' Sir George said. 'That seems a little ungrateful.'

'She was cruel to me, sir.' Again Janet was barely audible, as if the words were evoking memories she would rather forget.

'In what way?' Professor Sinclair probed.

'Beat me. Starved me. That is why I ran away.'

'I see,' said the Professor, 'you must have hated her.'

'We were very poor. She had little enough for herself,' Janet said. She paused, then added, almost under her breath so that the listeners strained to hear. 'She let others abuse me.'

'For payment?' the Professor asked gently.

The girl did not reply but sank back in the chair, obviously disturbed. The two men exchanged a look. The Professor gave Janet a few minutes to compose herself before he continued. 'Have you any knowledge of religion, Janet?'

'None, sir. I am ignorant of its principles . . . though I know the Lord's Prayer slightly.'

'Where did you learn that?'

'I didn't, sir, but I heard the witches repeat it in my dream. Then they changed the words to make it honour Satan.'

'Witches?' Sir George asked.

'Jenny Mathie was not alone. She acted with others,' the girl said firmly.

'Do you communicate with the Devil or any other spirit?' Sinclair asked sternly.

'No, sir. But the Devil is represented to me when I see the evil work of witches. I see him in the same shape and habit as they do.'

'If we may turn to the business of Sir George's illness.'

Sinclair said. 'How did you know that Jenny Mathie had bewitchit Sir George here?'

'I saw it, sir.'

'By what means?' Sinclair persisted.

'In a vision.'

'What exactly did you see in this vision?' Sinclair probed. Both men could see that the young girl was becoming slightly agitated. Her words came rapidly, almost like an incantation.

'I saw Jenny Mathie make a waxen image in which she stuck pins. I saw her calling on the devil to punish Sir George. I saw her hiding the likeness o' Sir George behind the fireplace.' She stopped, trembling.

'It is all richt lass. Nae need to be feart.' Sinclair said soothingly. 'The perpetrator is ahint bars. She cannot harm you.'

But Janet did not seem to hear him. Her eyes were wild, disturbed. She held up her hand warningly and continued.

'There are others who follow in her wake. They invoke the crooked Serpent. They walk hand in hand with Satan. They will carry out his will. They must be stopped!'

She let out a chilling cry and rushed to the window. 'I see him. I see him!'

'Whom do you see Janet?' Professor Sinclair asked urgently. 'What do you see?'

'I see the son of Jenny Mathie. He is in league with the evil one, the Prince of Darkness. He has a clay image of a man in his hand.' She turned to them frantically, 'Stop him! Stop him! He is casting it into the fire!'

Sinclair had been so intent on Janet's words that he did not see Sir George clutching at his throat throughout. There was a sudden crash as he hit the floor, dropping his claret glass into the fireplace. It broke on impact, scattering shards of glass everywhere. Sinclair rushed over to him, but he was pale and motionless. He looked at Janet in alarm but she was staring fixedly ahead. The Professor bent quickly over his friend and loosened the clothing around his neck.

'Sir George, speak to me, man. For the Lord's sake, say something.' He felt for a pulse but could find none. 'Do something, woman! For pity's sake . . . fetch Dr Bremner!'

But Janet did not seem to hear him. She remained gazing into the distance. Sinclair ran to the door calling loudly. 'Help, help! Dr Bremner! Come quick!'

When he turned back there was no sign of Janet. She must have slipped quietly out by the door on the far side of the room. He was relieved when at last the doctor appeared running along the corridor towards him.

Chapter Seven

Warlock

John Stewart drummed his fingers impatiently on his rough hewn kitchen table. Despite the jug of ale he was consuming, and the ones that had disappeared down his throat earlier 'to steady his nerve' as he told himself, he was still feeling uneasy. He wondered if he was wise staying on at his house in The Shaws, the locals' name for the village of Pollokshaws. Its proximity to the castle at Pollok worried him. He looked over at his young sister Annabil who was scurrying about making him a meal and felt a surge of resentment. Why him? Why had he been given this responsibility? Could his sister Mary not look after the girl? Annabil had been upset at the idea of going to live with Mary in

Glasgow. She wanted to be near their mother's house, to be able to visit her in prison. The girl was distraught at her arrest. John was never really close to his mother. He could not remember her ever giving him praise or encouragement as a child, always too ready with a tongue-lashing for his shortcomings. He knew, however, that she had nothing to do with the so called 'bewitching' of Sir George Maxwell. His mother had too much common sense to get involved in all that nonsense. The Maxwell family were just being vindictive, getting back at him, through her, for breaking into their orchards. The fact that it was some time ago was of no import. These people had long memories. He had heard through Will the herdsman, who had been present in the Great Hall of Pollok when the accusations of witch-craft had been made, that his name had been bandied about. John's instinct was to flee again, but it was not so easy with a fourteen year old sister in tow. The resentment building within him came out in a snarl. 'Hurry up! I'm stervin'!'

'I'm goin' as fast as I can John,' the young girl said apologetically.

Annabil had always been slightly in awe of her brother. Although, at sixteen, he was only two years older than her, he looked and behaved like a grown man. He was powerfully built, lived in his own house and earned a wage, though not always honestly, from what she had heard.

'Weel its no' fast enough. If I've to wait much longer you'll ken a' aboot it! A man works his airse aff a' day an' expects a meal waitin' for him.' His words were interrupted by a belch. The ale on an empty stomach was taking its toll. 'If ony lad's daft enough to wed you,' he continued, 'then you'll hae to sharpen your ideas. Whit hae you been dain aw day?'

'I went ower to oor ain hoose tae gie it a bit dicht,' the young girl explained. 'I want it to be shinin' for Mother comin' oot the jail.'

'If the talk's to be believit,' said John bluntly, 'she'll no' be comin' oot.'

Annabil's face crumpled. 'Whit hae you heard, John? Tell me!'

'Weel they say Ramsay, yon puffed up mannie, cries himsel' 'Commissioner for Witchcraft', aye gets a conviction.'

'But Mother has done nothing,' said Annabil anxiously, 'there are some aroon here dabble in that sort o' thing, but no Mother.'

John jumped up from the table and faced her angrily. 'Whit sort o' thing are you talkin' aboot?'

'Nothin',' said Annabil quickly. She was frightened at the ferocity of her brother's tone.

John grabbed her by the shoulders. 'Just you keep your mooth shut, you hear?' he shouted. 'That kinna talk is dangerous.'

'I've said nothin to naebody,' Annabil assured him nervously.

'Weel make sure you keep it that wey.' He released his grip. Annabil scurried away to the pot hanging over the fire. She ladled a generous portion of rabbit stew into a bowl and placed it in front of her brother.

'Aboot time,' he said, giving it a sniff. He took a cautious mouthful. She looked anxiously over at him.

'No' bad . . . no' bad.' He smacked his lips appreciatively. 'You bide wi' me much longer, sister, an' we'll mak a proper cook o' ye.'

Annabil was not interested in compliments. Her concerns were of a more serious nature. She had not forgotten that Janet Douglas had also pointed an accusatory finger at her.

'John, what did you mean about the Commissioner aye getting a conviction?' she asked, fearfully. 'Mother will never confess. She's done nothing.'

John paused between mouthfuls. 'Then they'll duck her in the river till she droons.'

'They canna dae that to an innocent person.' Annabil was clearly distressed.

A more considerate brother would have tempered his words, but tact and consideration were not part of John Stewart's make-up. 'Oh, they will declare her innocent, after she droons. That's their wey. If she floats, she's a witch an' they burn her. If she sinks, she's innocent. Fat lot o' good it'll dae her wi her lungs fu' o' watter.'

There was a sudden thunderous knocking at the door. John lowered his voice. 'Who the hell is that?'

Annabil's face broke into a smile. 'Maybe it's Mother. Maybe they've let her oot.' She rushed to the front door, but before she could reach the handle, it was pushed open with some force. She backed off in alarm as two men, armed with pikes, entered the room. Thomas Ramsay stood beside them, taking in the room and its occupants. Annabil felt a wave of fear come over her as she recognised Janet Douglas standing behind him. John Stewart rose to his feet.

'Whit's goin' on? Who the hell are you?'

Ramsay motioned to the two armed men who quickly moved to either side of Stewart, their pikes pointed menacingly in his direction. 'I will ask the questions here,' Ramsay said sharply.

Annabil cowered, petrified, in the corner.

'You are John Stewart, son of Jonit Mathie Stewart?' asked Ramsay.

'Who wants to know?' Stewart demanded defiantly.

Ramsay nodded to the younger of the armed men, who immediately hit Stewart in the ribs with the butt of his pike. John fell to the floor, grimacing in pain.

'I do not think you are listening, Master Stewart,' Ramsay said over his shoulder. He was now focussing on Annabil. 'You are Annabil Stewart, sister of this stubborn fellow?'

'Y . . . yes, sir.' The young girl was clearly terrified.

'How old are you Annabil?' the Commissioner asked.

'Fourteen, sir.'

Ramsay turned back to her brother, still recovering from the blow. 'You see, Stewart, how polite, how co-operative your sister is. That is what I want from you. Now you asked who I was and although you did not ask it ower nicely, I will tell you. The name is Thomas Ramsay, Commissioner for Witchcraft.'

A slight gasp of fear escaped Annabil's lips. Ramsay immediately wheeled back towards her. 'Why so feart m'dear? Surely you have nothing to hide. Have you?'

'N . . . no sir.'

He put his face close to hers, menacingly. 'Yet it is my experience that if one member of a family practises that evil diabolic art which I am pledgit to destroy, then others of that breed may be similarly infectit.'

'No, no . . . not me sir.' The young girl was on the verge of tears.

Ramsay spun round to face John. He motioned to the pikesmen, who pulled Stewart to his feet. 'And what about you John? Although your mother has not yet confessit we hae enough evidence to burn her for witchcraft.'

A sob broke from Annabil. She looked over at Janet Douglas, still standing quietly in the corner. The girl returned the look with an inscrutable expression.

Ramsay drew closer to John. He could smell the ale on the young man's breath. 'Now, what tricks did you learn at your mother's knee, John, eh?'

'I dinna ken what you're talking about.' Stewart's tone was still defiant.

'Now, now, man, dinna blacken your soul ony further,' Ramsay said. 'The talk in the Shaws is . . . you're a war-lock!'

'That is nonsense!' John answered scornfully. 'I'm nae mair guilty than my mother!'

'A poor defence, John.' Ramsay's tone was deceptively smooth. 'If we have to save you from the same fate as has befallit your mother, then we best check oot your story. I take it you have nae objection if we search your premises?'

'Go ahead,' said John defiantly. 'I hae nothin' to hide.'

The Commissioner smiled, a smile that failed to reach his eyes.

'Is that not touching? I do believe your mother usit the self same words.'

He gestured to the two armed men who started turning the place over, pulling everything from a small cabinet and strewing the contents on the floor. The younger one swept the few cooking ingredients from a shelf, breaking bowls and containers in the process. They found nothing. Janet Douglas walked over to the Commissioner and pointed to the bed.

'Oh no!' The words came from Annabil. She was visibly shaking, having witnessed the same procedure at her mother's house.

'John Stewart . . . come ower here and light a candle,' Ramsay ordered. John opened his tinder box, struck a flint and lit a candle. He seemed cocksure, unconcerned.

'Now if we find onything here as Janet Douglas has foreseen,' Ramsay said in an officious voice, 'I want nae talk o' collusion. Janet, awa and stand in the far corner ower there. Annabil, you go with her.'

The two girls crossed to the corner, Annabil eyeing the other warily. Janet's expression gave nothing away.

'Now I call on you men, James Grant and Ludowick Frazer of Househill, to witness that Janet Douglas is far removit from this bed. What say ye?'

'Aye sir,' the two men chorused.

'Come nearer, John Stewart,' Ramsay ordered. With all the nonchalance he could muster, Stewart sauntered towards him.

'Right!' said Ramsay. 'You may proceed.'

The two men pulled back the bedclothes and started looking amongst the bedstraw. Ludowick lifted the bolster and straightened up, clutching a small clay effigy which had been lying concealed amongst the straw. He held it up triumphantly, 'Commissioner!'

'Bring it ower!' Ramsay ordered.

Ludowick handed it over carefully. 'Be careful sir! 'Tis fresh made, and liable to break.'

'Well, well, look here gentlemen,' Ramsay smiled grimly. 'Witness this. James what do you see?'

'A clay likeness sir,' the other man stated.

'What else do you see, Ludowick?'

'Three pins in the figure, sir.'

'Where be they placit?' he asked James.

'Two in the side and one in the breest.'

'You hear that Stewart, before two independent witnesses? What have you to say for yourself?'

Stewart, looking totally confused, said nothing.

'Come, come Master Stewart. Are we to take it that your silence is an admission of guilt?'

'Somebody must have pit it there,' said John, perplexed.

'Now, my mannie, you can do better than that.' Ramsay smiled his grim smile once again. 'Your ain mother used that yin.'

'I tell ye. I ken nothin' aboot it,' John's tone was now anxious, insistent. The seriousness of the situation was finally dawning on him.

'Oh, I think a wee spell in the prison hoose o' Paisley may loosen your tongue.' Ramsay's tone changed to one of formality as he announced the charge.

'John Stewart of Pollokshaws, on the authority of the Earl of Dundonald and Lord Ross of His Majesty's Privy Council, I herefore arrest you for the crime of sorcery.'

John was silent, stunned.

Ramsay turned his attention to Annabil, now so drained of colour that she looked as if she was about to faint. 'Annabil Stewart, have you anything to say of your part in this matter?'

'I ken nothing,' she whispered.

'Yet you seemed to ken there was something under that bolster?' Ramsay said accusingly.

Annabil started to cry, tears running down her cheeks.

'I hae seen ower mony witches' tears to be movit,' said Ramsay dismissively. 'Take them away!'

The two men marched Stewart and Annabil off at pike point. A crowd of curious neighbours who had gathered outside drew back, talking amongst themselves, wondering if the law had caught up with the light fingered Stewart at long last.

Ramsay turned to Janet. 'Miss Douglas, it appears His Majesty's Privy Council is once again indebtit to you.'

He followed the prisoners out. Janet looked round the cottage and turned back, a strange little half-smile playing on her lips.

Chapter Eight

Witch-pricking

Although news in the Shaws and Polloktoun was that Sir George Maxwell was only just clinging to life for the second time, the subject on everyone's lips was the arrest of Jenny Mathie's son, John, her daughter Annabil, sister-in-law Margaret Jackson and neighbours Bessie Weir and Margery Craige. Fear was running high in both villages. Who would be the next to be arrested for witchcraft?

Meanwhile all those arrested for the bewitching of Sir George Maxwell had been subjected to the humiliation of being stripped and searched for witches' marks. Any wart, birthmark, skin tag, or other excrescence was seen as evidence of sorcery. A team of investigators, headed by Thomas Ramsay, probed and pricked each prisoner's skin, looking for areas insensitive to pain. Any found were declared Devil's marks, given to them when they declared allegiance to Satan. All but fourteen year old Annabil were declared to be carrying the marks. The young girl screamed from the moment she was stripped naked. The others, like Jenny, half dead from the tortures they had already endured, were barely aware of what was going on.

Thomas Ramsay was enjoying a well earned break, supping a jar of ale and eating fresh baked bread and cheese. It had been a busy day and a successful one. That Annabil Stewart was free of marks did not trouble him. Because of her youth, it was unlikely she would be burned at the stake, but, in her state of terror, she had been easily persuaded to name and indict others, her family and neighbours and they, with the exception of Jenny Mathie, were now ready to break. However, Ramsay had plans to remedy her mother's obstinacy. He was interrupted in his mood of self-congratulation when one of the gaolers appeared.

'Beggin' your pardon, sir, but yin o' the prisoners wishes to see you.'

'Who is it?'

'Margery Craige sir, yin o' the witches.'

'Do you ken what she wants?'

'Aye sir, she's beggin' to be swum.'

Ramsay rose to his feet, irritated. There was no way he was going to accede to her request. He strode along to her cell, the gaoler in tow. Margery Craige, a middle aged, work worn woman, was lying there manacled, shivering and naked.

'What is this nonsense about swimming?'

'Please sir, I beg you to let me be swum. I'm so fearit o' the flames.'

'Are you indeed? You ken that you would be tied up, unable to swim, when you are thrown in?'

'Aye sir, but I am no' afraid o' that.'

'Because you are a witch and ken that you will float? Am I richt?'

'No sir.'

'No indeed. You are hoping that you will trick us into letting you drown.'

'If the guid Lord Jesus decrees that, I am ready to face Him.'

He crossed to her, struck her, hard, across the face.

'How dare you say the name o' the Lord when you are in a pact with Satan.'

Blood trickled from the woman's mouth where his blow had struck.

'You will burn at the stake with the rest of your accomplices.'

The wretched woman started to sob.

'But if you confess,' he continued, 'you will be hangit before your miserable body is consignit to the flames. Think on it.'

Before the woman could say anything in reply, Ramsay was interrupted by a piercing scream from a nearby cell. He smiled.

'Sounds as if my assistant has found a way of breaching

83

Jenny Mathie's stubbornness. Perhaps, now, even she will confess.'

He turned on his heel, leaving the gaoler to lock the cell door, strode down the corridor and entered Jenny Mathie's cell. A smell of singed flesh greeted him. Her gaoler nodded to Ramsay, indicating the W clearly burnt on the unfortunate woman's left shoulder. The Reverend William Reid, Chaplain to the prison, was mouthing prayers over her.

'She has passit oot wi' the pain,' Ramsay's assistant said, in a matter of fact voice.

'We'll soon remedy that.' Ramsay picked up a jug of water and threw it into the unconscious woman's face.

She came to, spluttering and wincing with pain, to see Ramsay standing over her.

'Weel, Mistress Stewart . . . are you ready to confess to your paction wi' Satan? You only hae to say the word and my freen here will leave you in peace.'

'Peace to be burnit at the stake.' Jenny's voice was hoarse, but defiant, despite her obvious distress.

'Come, come, Jenny, we widna be sae hasty,' Ramsay said smoothly. 'We hae mony fair trials for you to undergo afore we reach that happy release.'

'I ken aboot your trials,' Jennie said faintly. 'They aye hae the same conclusion.'

'Confess and repent, Jonet Mathie. It is not too late,' Reverend Reid urged. His stomach was still a little queasy from the smell of singed flesh. He had never become inured to branding, though he had witnessed it many times. He was always anxious, in carrying out God's work, to see these cases to a swift conclusion.

'The Lord can stop Satan's fury and hinder him in his design,' he continued. 'Free yourself from the devil's yoke.'

'I've done nothin',' Jenny answered wearily. 'How lang dae I hae to keep tellin' you that?'

'Till you hae a chynge o' heart and speak the truth.' Ramsay was losing patience.

'I am innocent,' she insisted.

The Commissioner thrust a wax doll in front of her.

'Then how dae you explain this awa?'

'I ken nothin' o' this.'

'Then how would it come to be hidden awa in a secret place ahint your fireplace?'

'I have telt ye a hunnert times,' she replied, 'it was the deed o' the dumb girl, Janet Douglas. She pit it there.'

Ramsay put his face very close to hers.

'Sir George's twa servants, James Dunlop and Laurence Martin . . . honest men baith . . . swearit on oath, on oath mind ye, that Janet Douglas was naewhere near your fireplace. Are you sayin' they are liars tae?'

'She pit it there I tell ye!' Jenny insisted.

'Perhaps you can tell us how?'

'I dinna ken. She has powers I canna understand. It is her you should be questionin', nae me. I widnae herm Sir George!'

'Then how do you explain his miraculous recovery

when we removit the pins frae this doll found in your dwelling place?'

'I dinna ken,' the woman said wearily.

'Oh, I think you ken mair than you are saying, Jenny Mathie.' Ramsay's voice was quietly menacing. 'Satan has powers that canna be explainit . . . especially when he has the help o' a willing accomplice.'

'Sir, if I may be so bold to suggest?' his assistant interrupted.

'Yes, William, you have another little device for loosening lockit tongues?'

'I have many sir, but this one is stubborn. I ken the type, but her daughter is here. Her marrit daughter fae Glasgow. She's been waitin' all mornin', demandin' to see her mother. Perhaps we micht enlist her aid?'

Ramsay reflected for a moment. 'Why not, William?'

He turned to the gaoler. 'Show her in.' He quickly raised the shoulder of Mathie's gown, concealing the scorched flesh.

The man disappeared for a few moments before returning with Mary Robertson and a tall, thin figure in clerical dress. The Commissioner's assistant let the woman enter, but barred the way of the cleric. 'Just a minute, my mannie. Whit are you dain' here?'

'It is all richt William,' Ramsay's smooth tone was coupled with a hint of wariness. 'Weel, weel, the Reverend Mr Bell, if I am not mistaken. To what do we owe this dubious honour?'

'I askit him to come here,' Mary Robertson interjected.

'He kens your ways.' She looked in disbelief at the poor pathetic woman manacled to the wall, a pale shadow of what her mother had been.

'Whit hae you done to her?' she asked tearfully.

'Nothing yet my dear. We are merely trying to find the truth o' this unfortunate affair,' the Commissioner answered. 'Look . . . see for yoursel'! Your mother is as obstinate as ever.'

'Mother, it's me! Open your eyes, Mother! It's Mary. Tell me you're aw richt.' The woman gently wiped the hair away from her mother's eyes. All colour seemed to have drained from the older woman's face.

'She is exhaustit, Mary. They hae deprivit her o' sleep,' Reverend Bell explained. 'It is yin o' their ploys.'

'D'ye hear that Mr Reid?' the Commissioner addressed the Prison Chaplain. 'The Reverend Bell thinks he is something of an expert in oor ways.'

'I am familiar with his publication,' Reid replied. 'He is a disgrace to the cloth!'

'More than that,' Ramsay continued, 'he is a danger to his flock. Anyone who defends witches seems, to me, to be hand in hand with Satan.'

If he'd tried to provoke the Reverend Bell, he'd succeeded.

'If you had read my treatise properly, you'd be aware that I speak out only against injustice!' Bell answered angrily. 'You ken how much harm has been done to worthy and innocent people like Jenny Mathie here. You ken that old age, poverty, ill-looks and groundless fears are enough for some folk to defame their neighbours to the unspeakable prejudice of Christian charity. I have known Jenny Mathie for years. I admit she has made some enemies by the sharpness o' her tongue, but she would no more consort wi' Satan than I would.'

Jenny opened her eyes. 'Listen to him. He speaks the truth.' Her voice was a whisper.

The Commissioner turned on Bell menacingly, 'You are not preaching at your Conventicles now, Mr Bell. You'll find I'm made of less gullible mettle.'

The Reverend Bell started. It was his turn to look wary.

'Did I startle you there Reverend? I hope I didnae frighten you.' Ramsay came right up to him, menacingly.

'You surely realise, do you not, that it is only a matter o' time before all you Covenanters are roundit up? Next time you are preachin' oot there in the fields, you had better keep glancin' ower your shoulder.'

'If you think you are going to silence me with your threats, then you are wrong,' Bell met the Commissioner's gaze defiantly. 'They will hae to rip out ma tongue afore I stop speakin' against the burnin' o' innocent people and the torturin o' poor folk of more goodness and esteem than most of their calumniators.'

'Dinna give me your self-righteous indignation, Reverend,' Ramsay almost spat out the words, 'I am merely doin' my job.'

'I believe Pontius Pilate offert the same excuse,' Bell answered.

Chapter Nine

The Visitor

Margaret was surprised and delighted to see her father out of bed and dressed. She thought she had lost him on the night of his collapse, following the dinner party. Professor Sinclair seemed to believe that finding the clay image at John Stewart's house had led to his recovery. Margaret wondered if the improvement in his health was, perhaps, due more to the imminent return of her mother and the family from their London sojourn. They were due to arrive home the following day. Judging from her letter, Lady Maxwell had seen behind the carefully chosen words in Margaret's missive, and was distraught with worry about her husband. Sir George was anxious to alleviate her fears. He did not wish his wife to see a bed-ridden invalid. He had forced down the nutritious meals which Margaret brought him, obediently swallowed the physic prescribed by Doctor Bremner and, though not entirely recovered, gained something of his former strength. When he proposed joining Margaret on a walk in the fresh air, however, she dissuaded him. There was a biting January wind which chilled to the very bone. He felt restless, trapped and anxious to be doing something. When Laurence announced a visitor, by the name of Mary Robertson, Sir George, delighted at the diversion, asked that she be shown in. Laurence warned that she was a relative of the Stewarts, those responsible for his illness. Sir George hesitated for a moment, then asked that she be shown up when Miss Margaret returned. Laurence suggested that, given the circumstances, it might be more prudent to turn the woman away. His master dismissed the servant's fears. Aspects of the case against the Stewarts worried Sir George. He felt this woman had a right to be heard.

When Margaret, who had been out walking in the grounds, heard of the visitor she was alarmed. She rushed to the Master of the Household's office where Janet Douglas was employed assisting with the accounts. The position of under house-maid, which Janet held briefly, had seemed inappropriate to one of her education. She now assisted Robert Fraser by copying the household and estate accounts in a neat hand. The office was empty. According to the servants, the girl was out on estate business with Fraser, but was expected to return shortly. Margaret made her way quickly to the drawing room to join her father.

'Do you think it is wise to receive this woman Father?' she asked.

'The Reverend Bell's letter has raised doubts in my mind,' Sir George answered worriedly. 'It is only right that I am acquaintit with all the facts. Perhaps this woman can throw further light on the matter. I have no wish to have the blood o' innocent folk on my hands.'

There was a discreet knock on the door. The servant, Laurence, ushered in a buxom, handsome woman in her late thirties.

'Mary Robertson, Sir George,' he announced.

Margaret started in surprise. The woman seemed very familiar to her, but she could not remember where they had met. Laurence remained by the door in watchful attendance.

'Thank you, Laurence. You may leave us,' said Sir George.

'But, Sir,' Laurence protested. He saw the look on his employer's face, one that brooked no argument. 'I will be outside the door if you need me.' He directed his remark threateningly at the woman, who seemed anxious, on edge. As the door closed behind him, there was a pause, broken by Sir George.

'My servants seem to think I have something to fear from you Mistress Robertson. Is that so?' he asked.

'No, indeed. I swear not sir. You ken who I am?'

'The daughter of Jenny Mathie Stewart, and sister to

Annabil and John, at present in custody for attemptit injury to my person, through paction wi' the devil,' he said pointedly.

'It is untrue, sir,' the woman said earnestly. 'My family hae nothing agin you. Nor have they ony truck wi' witchcraft.'

'My household is of a different opinion,' said Sir George. 'They urged me not to see you. I feel, though, if you have come all the way from Glasgow you may be able to throw some light on this wretchit business.'

'I've been waiting for twa days to see you. The river was so swelt up I couldna get across to your hoose afore now. Sir George, my family are innocent. I beg you to help them,' she pleaded.

It was then Margaret remembered where she had seen Mary Robertson before. She was the sweetmeat seller from the Glasgow Fair. How odd, she thought. What a strange coincidence that this woman was the daughter of Jenny Mathie. She felt suddenly wary, afraid again for her father. If he shared her concern, he showed no sign of it. He approached Mary Robertson, a stern expression on his face. 'You understand, do you not, that I was at death's very door until your family was arrestit? I am the last person you should ask.'

'But you kent my mother and father for many years. They spent a lifetime in your employ and served you faithfully,' the woman said, with real agitation in her voice. 'You must ken this is none of my mother's doing.'

'But what of your brother, John ?' Margaret interjected.

'My brother is a fool, Mistress, but he's nae warlock.'

'It appears your sister Annabil is of a different opinion,' said Sir George.

'Whit do you mean?' Mary Robertson asked fearfully.

'I mean that she has now confessit.'

'To what?'

'A paction with others to invoke the Devil's malice agin the family of Pollok,' Sir George replied gravely.

'It is not true,' the woman protested tearfully. 'What others? Who else did she name?'

'Your mother, brother and several neighbours who bide on my estate. Bessie Weir, Margery Craige and Margaret Jackson.'

'I canny believe this! Margaret Jackson is my aunt,' Mary said, distraught. 'She is a guid old woman, aye at the kirk. Why would Annabil give her name? Or any of the others? They are all decent God fearing women.'

'I must confess I found it difficult to grasp myself,' said Sir George but when the Depute Sheriff o' Renfrew himself witnessed the insensible marks on their person, I had to be convincit.'

'Insensible marks? You mean witches' marks?' asked Mary Roberson, fearfully.

'Aye lass. Your mother was covered in them.'

'She insists, yet, that she is innocent,' Margaret interjected, 'but when they found them on your brother, he broke doon and confessit.'

'It canna be.' Tears were now coursing down the woman's cheeks.

'There, there lass, I understand your feelings,' Sir George said solicitously, 'but perhaps you should be thankin' the guid Lord that you are merrit and awa from your family or you, too, might hae been taintit.'

'But it is not true,' Mary Robertson's tone was insistent. 'I tell you. It is her doing.'

'Who?' asked Margaret.

'Janet Douglas. She is responsible!' the woman said.

'Whit do you know of Janet Douglas?' Sir George asked.

'I met her at the Glesca Fair. She has powers I dinna understand. We took her in to bide with us for a few days when she had naewhere to go. Why is she doin' this to my family? We've done nothing to her.'

'So you truly believe she is behind this?' Margaret asked.

'I know she is. But I canna understand why.'

'Well, perhaps you should put that question to her yoursel,' said Sir George, who had glanced out of the window to see Janet Douglas and Robert Fraser crossing the yard. He strode to the door, calling for the servant. Laurence rushed in immediately.

'I'm here, Sir. Is everything a' richt?'

'Of course it is,' Sir George said smoothly. 'This lady doesna bite. Ask Janet to come here.' He turned back to Mary Robertson. 'Whatever your fears are on this matter let me assure you that your family will be given a fair trial.'

'The Reverend Bell says few get acquitit when they're accusit o' witchcraft,' Mary said worriedly.

'Although I hae great sympathy wi' the Reverend Bell and

his Covenanting cause, he's no entirely blameless on that score. Seems to me his fellow clergymen hae been first to the taper when witches were tried. They seem to see sorcery aw aroon them.'

'He's no' like that,' Mary said firmly.

'So I have been told. But neither are the men who will be trying your family and the other poor women. We hae some of the finest members of the judiciary in the land; Sir Patrick Gauston, James Brisbane of Bishopton, Sir John Shaw of Greenock and John Preston the Advocate. They have appointit Lord Ross as Judge Assessor with power to vote and decide. These men will no' be easily swayt. You can be assurit.'

He broke off as the door was tapped lightly and then opened. Janet Douglas stood in the doorway.

'Ah . . . Janet . . . I believe you ken Mistress Robertson.'

Janet looked coldly at Mary Robertson, but said nothing.

Mary Robertson crossed over to the girl. 'Why are you doing this to my family? What harm hae they done you?'

'They are guilty of witchcraft,' said Janet firmly.

'That is not true and you ken it,' said Mary brokenly.

'Janet,' Sir George interjected, 'how do you come to this knowledge of their witchcraft?'

'Because she is one hersel', that's how!' Mary said angrily.

Sir George held up a restraining hand. 'How did you know about these likenesses of me that brought me down so terribly?'

Margaret listened intently. Although her father had told

her the details of Professor Sinclair's interrogation, she wanted to hear the words directly from Janet. Six people's lives depended on the young girl's testimony.

'I saw it in a vision sir. It was revealit to me,' Janet answered.

'How can this be?' asked Margaret.

'I do not know, mistress. I know these things as if I were present at their happening. I saw the coven wi' Jenny Mathie and her son present. They consort with the evil one. They must be punished!'

'You liar!' said Mary Robertson angrily, rushing at Janet Douglas as if to grapple with her. Margaret and her father stood transfixed. They felt they should intervene, but there was no need. Janet Douglas let out an eerie cry and put a hand out towards Mary Robertson, stopping her in her tracks.

'Do not touch me, Daughter of Beelzebub,' she intoned. 'You are one of them!'

Margaret felt a cold chill run throughout her body. Janet seemed in almost a trance like state. Her eyes focussing on something not quite within the room, she uttered once again.

'I can see . . . you have consorted with the evil serpent. You lie with the Prince of Darkness. Sister of Satan, confess and repent for your end is nigh. You will plunge into the dark waters with your blackened soul. Confess and repent before it is too late.'

Sir George once again found his voice. 'What are you saying?'

Janet pointed her finger accusingly. 'I say Mary Roberson that you are a witch!'

'That is a lie!' Mary backed away from her, clearly distressed. 'Sir George dinna believe her. She speaks falsely.'

Janet moved swiftly across the room and with great force, ripped the collar from Mary's dress.

'See, she has the insensible mark! Do you deny now, Mary Robertson, the proof before your eyes? The mark which Satan put upon you. The mark of a witch?'

Mary let out a long anguished scream and ran from the room.

Sir George stood looking totally stunned. Margaret looked over at Janet, trying to read her expression, but it was impossible to fathom.

Chapter Ten

The Witchcraft Trial

There was an air of solemnity in the Court. Margaret was grateful for her brother's solid reassuring presence beside her. On completion of his law studies, John had been enjoying the grand tour of Europe, much to the envy of his young sister. Not for the first time did she wish she was born a man. The opportunities afforded to them seemed limitless. Margaret hung on his every word regarding the treasures and antiquities of Florence and Rome. He, on the other hand, felt that he should have been at home during his father's ordeal. Professor Sinclair had written informing him of the alleged bewitching of Sir George and his own subsequent examination of Janet Douglas. John had been visiting Ravenna in order to see its mosaics when the letter reached him. He returned home immediately.

He was in court in order to see justice done. Father's health seemed to be giving regular cause for alarm. His condition, according to his physician, was a chronic one. Sir George did not feel strong enough to attend the trial and was at home attended by Lady Maxwell. John and Margaret promised to convey all the court proceedings.

They had missed the morning session due to a sudden snow-fall and had waited till its passing before venturing out in the carriage. John was a little surprised that neither Margaret, nor Sir George, had been called as witnesses. Apparently, it had not been deemed necessary. Margaret recognised some of the villagers from Polloktoun amongst a rabble in the public gallery. She was reminded of her brother's vivid description of the Coliseum in Rome and the spectator sport it provided. She hoped and prayed that those who might be sacrificed in the arena of the Justice Court in Paisley truly deserved their fate.

On one side of the court sat the accused, Jenny Mathie Stewart, her son John, daughter Annabil, and sister-in-law Margaret Jackson, who, at eighty years of age, seemed more than a little confused as to what was happening. Alongside sat their co-accused, two neighbours, Bessie Weir and Margery Craige.

Margaret was shocked at the change in the appearance of Jenny Mathie, who had been a strong robust woman, despite her advanced years. She seemed a pale shadow of her former self. Perhaps the Reverend Bell was right in his claim that she had been tortured. She dismissed the idea immediately. This was a civilised society, not ancient Rome. She felt reassured when she saw the Defence Council, Sir Patrick Gauston, a man of unimpeachable reputation. There was a murmuring in the court. All rose for the arrival of the Presiding Judge, Lord Ross. The Prosecuting Advocate, John Preston, called Laurence Martin, Sir George's man-servant, to the witness box. Laurence had confided to Margaret before he left for Paisley that he had not slept a wink the night before. She reassured him that all he needed to do was tell the truth.

'Then the witches might come after me,' he had said fearfully.

The young girl was concerned that he had already made up his mind about their guilt. It was hoped that the skills of the Defence Council would prevent any bias in his testimony. John Preston, the Prosecuting Council, rose to his feet and, after the preliminaries, began his questioning.

'Mr Martin, would you tell the court, in your own words, what happened on your visit to the house of the accusit, Jonet Mathie Stewart, known as Jenny, in Polloktoun on the third of November last.'

Despite his apprehension, Laurence spoke up loudly and clearly as Margaret had advised.

'Well sir, we, that is, James Dunlop and myself went along to Jenny Mathie's house accompanit by Janet Douglas and demandit to search her dwelling.'

'Did you give a reason for your search?' the Prosecutor asked.

'Not at first, sir. We didnae want to pit her on guard.'

That wasn't quite true thought Margaret. Janet Douglas had shown the drawing of the figure, stabbed with pins, in front of Jenny Mathie that day in the Great Hall of Pollok. Jenny knew why they were searching. Fortunately, Gauston, the Defence Council, rose to challenge Laurence's statement.

'M'Lord. Surely the witness is inferring the accusit had something to hide?'

'Indeed.' The Judge looked reprovingly over his spectacles at Laurence. 'Witness will confine himself to the question,' he said. Laurence looked suitably chastened as the Prosecutor continued.

'What did Mistress Mathie say to your request?'

'She telt me where to go, Sir.'

'I take it, by this, she did not mean Pollokshaws?' the Prosecutor asked smiling.

'No, sir. I mean she swore,' Laurence explained.

Again Margaret wondered if Laurence was embellishing the truth. She distinctly remembered Jenny Mathie inviting them to search as she left the Great Hall. Her last words were that she had nothing to hide.

'What did you do then?' asked the Prosecutor.

'We explainit that she was under suspicion for the bewitching of Sir George Maxwell and if she wantit to clear her name she should let us search her dwelling.'

'And she let you in?'

'Yes sir. She said she had nothing to hide.'

At least that was true, thought Margaret thankfully.

'Please confine yourself to the question, Mr Martin,' the Prosecutor chided.

'Sorry, sir.'

'Would you tell us in your own words what happened next?'

'Well sir, I stood beside Mistress Mathie while James . . . Mr Dunlop searchit ahint the fireplace. He then found a waxen figure with three pins placit in it, which we took awa.'

'Did you observe Janet Douglas during the finding of the waxen object?'

'Aye sir.'

'Where was she in the room?'

'She was near the fireplace, sir.'

'How near?'

'Oh . . . aboot twa arm lengths distant.'

'I see. Would it have been possible for her to place anything behind the fireplace?'

Gauston, the Defence Council, rose to his feet. 'This is conjecture, M'Lord'.

'An important point, however,' muttered the Judge. 'Mr Martin, you may answer the question.'

'Nae withoot my observin' it, sir,' said Laurence.

'And did you see her place anything there?' the Prosecutor persisted.

'No sir. I watchit her and she didna move.'

102

Jenny Mathie rose to her feet, furious. 'She pit it there I tell you. She's the one wha should be on trial, nae me.'

Margaret was taken aback at the ferocity of Jenny's accusation.

Despite her wasted appearance, her voice was clear and firm.

'Jonet Mathie, you are not helping your case by showing disrespect to the Court,' said the Judge gravely. 'If you interrupt proceedings again I will have you ejectit fae the room.'

'One final question, M' Lord,' said the Prosecutor. 'Mr Martin, you told us earlier of the poor state of Sir George's health prior to your visit to Mistress Mathie. What was his state of health after you returnit and removit the pins from the effigy found there?'

'It was miraculous, sir. The colour had returnit to his cheeks and he was like his old self again.'

John looked at Margaret questioningly.

'He's overstating it,' Margaret whispered.

'Thank you, Mr Martin. No further questions,' said the Prosecutor.

'Mr Gauston, do you wish to question the witness?'

The Defence Council shook his head. Margaret was surprised. There were a few questions she would like to have put to Laurence. It was obvious he had decided Jenny Mathie was guilty.

'You may step down, Mr Martin,' the Judge instructed.

The Clerk of the Court rose to his feet. 'I call Annabil Stewart to the witness stand.'

Annabil rose. She was pale and visibly trembling.

'May I remind the witness that she is still on oath,' said the Judge. The Prosecutor rose to his feet once again.

'You are Annabil Stewart, daughter of Jonit Mathie Stewart?'

'Yes, sir,' she said faintly.

'Miss Stewart, I would like you to tell the court, in your own words, of the events which happened on Harvest last, when you returnit to your mother's house to find three of the accused here present.'

'Well. sir, on Harvest last I came home from my work on Sir George Maxwell's estate to find Bessie Weir, Margery Craige and Margaret Jackson all present at Mother's house . . . '

'Would you please speak up, Miss Stewart,' the Judge commanded.

Annabil nodded apologetically before continuing. 'I had been at home but five minutes when . . . when . . . the Devil appearit, and demandit that I give myself to him. I did not want to do this for I was feart. The Devil was all in black and he scarit me. . . . My mother said if I did as he requestit I would get a new coat and the Devil was very nice to me. Telt me to call him Ejoal and promisit me onythin' I wantit. Instructit by my mother and the other women present, I pit ma hand to the crown o' my head and the other to the soul of my foot and did give myself up to him. After that the Devil lay abed with me under the clothes.'

There was a muttering in the court. The Judge banged

his gavel and Annabil continued, 'I wantit him to stay away for he was cold, but he placed me nearest to him. When I awoke, Bessie Weir was turning a waxen image on a spit before the fire. The Devil, Bessie Weir, Margery Craige, Margaret Jackson and my mother, Jenny Mathie, all repeatit the name "Sir George Maxwell" as she turnit.'

Margaret looked at her brother in astonishment. Could this be true?

Despite Annabil's initial hesitancy, there was a sense of what she had just said being, somehow, rehearsed. Had this 'confession' been forced from her? Margaret had heard rumours of confessions being extracted under torture. Annabil Stewart looked so terrified that she seemed totally compliant, giving the Prosecutor what he wanted to hear. Her mother, Margaret noticed, just sat there, shaking her head in disbelief.

Twenty minutes later when it was the turn of John Stewart, Jenny's son to give evidence, Margaret felt the same nagging doubt. The youth, initially, was monosyllabic, but questioned about satanic intervention, spoke with a fluency that appeared unreal. Had he, too, been tutored in what to say? There was nasty purple bruising above his eye but no-one seemed to question him about that. What other injuries had been inflicted upon him? wondered Margaret. Would the authorities allow this to happen? According to her brother, although they claimed to be against the use of torture, they conveniently failed to denounce abuses of the system. John Stewart broke off to have a sip of liquid, then continued. Margaret listened very attentively to what he had to say.

'On Wednesday, the third of January last, I had just gone to bed when I heard someone call me by name. I awoke and saw a man there dressit in black wi' bluish handcuffs. He had hoggers on his legs and was without shoes. When he spoke, his voice was hough and goustie and I kent him to be the Devil. I lit a candle and found that Bessie Weir, Margaret Jackson and Margery Craige had already enterit my house through the window. They said that they had invokit the Devil's help to avenge the taking of my mother Jenny Mathie, who was at that time in the Paisley Jail. The Devil askit me to renounce my baptism and said in return I should not want for any pleesure. After placing yin hand on my head and the other on the soul of my foot I was gien the spirit name "Jonas". The Devil askit oor consent for the making of an effigy to tak away the life o' Sir George Maxwell o' Pollok.'

Margaret's brother squeezed her hand comfortingly as John Stewart continued.

'The women wrought the clay and the Devil made the face, hands and legs. I held the candle while he did this and saw by its light that his feet were cloven. While the Devil was placing three pins in the clay figure, my sister, Annabil came to the house and remainit during the proceedings.'

After a short recess, Margaret Jackson, sister-in-law to Jenny Mathie was called to the witness stand. At eighty years of age although sprightly enough in her walk, she seemed bewildered to find herself in this position. Yet when she was questioned about consorting with the devil, again Margaret was surprised by the old woman's fluency. It was as if all three were singing from the same demonic hymn book.

'I am Margaret Jackson relict of the late Thomas Jackson of Pollokshaws,' she said, in a loud, but quavering voice. 'Bessie Weir came to me for help in obtaining her revenge on Sir George Maxwell of Pollok. Sir George had refusit to enter her husband in his harvest service and causit her bairns to hae little to live on as a consequence. Bessie kent that my acquaintance wi' the devil went further back than hers. Some forty years ago he first came to me when I was at Pollokshaws-croft, carrying a few sticks on my back. He offert to carry them for me and said he could lighten my load permanent-like, if I gave myself to him. I renouncit my baptism and was given the name "Locas". On the third of January last I woke up and found a man in my bed. I thought at first it was my husband but he has been dead twenty years or therebye. I kent then it was the devil and he telt me to form a paction wi' Jenny Mathie Stewart and her family together with Bessie Weir and Margery Craige, the purpose o' which was to bring aboot the daith o' Sir George Maxwell o' Pollok. We met and agreeit to this.'

Jenny Mathie Stewart rose to her feet angrily. 'It's aw lies. I ken nothin' o this. They've been forcit to say this. It is not true!'

'Mistress Mathie,' the Judge said gravely. 'I have already warnit you about interrupting court proceedings. I have no alternative but to ban you from the court herewith. Take her away.'

A man, armed with a pike, grasped her roughly by the arm and escorted her from the room. Her shouts resounded through the court as she was being led away.

'It is Janet Douglas's doing. She's the yin you should be trying. She's foolit the lot o' ye!'

Margaret found it hard to believe that Janet Douglas, so fundamental to these charges being brought, had not been called as a witness, particularly as the Judge was drawing the proceedings to a close.

'Milords of the Privy Council,' he began gravely 'you have heard the evidence before you and the confessions of John Stewart, Annabil Stewart, Margery Craige, Bessie Weir and Margaret Jackson, to the bewitching of Sir George Maxwell of Pollok. Only Jonit Mathie Stewart remains stubborn in her obstinacy. However, we have heard evidence from her gaoler at Paisley prison who swore, on oath, that though Mathie's feet were fixit in the stocks, she had movit those stocks six yards in order to obtain a bolster for her head. Bear in mind that twa of the strongest men in the country could barely lift them, and consider, if you need, that this is further evidence of her sorcery. She has, by some, been branded a witch for many years.'

Margaret exchanged a puzzled look with her brother. If the latter was true, why had it not reached the ears of the Maxwell family.

'Although,' the Judge continued, 'this is often the case

with innocent people of mature years, particularly those who carry out the function of midwife. However, conclusive proof, if such you require, is the finding of many insensible marks, commonly known as witches' marks upon her person. I therefore find Jonit Mathie Stewart, John Stewart, Bessie Weir, Margaret Jackson, Margery Craige and Annabil Stewart all guilty of witchcraft.'

Annabil Stewart started to sob as did Bessie Weir. John Stewart turned pale but did not make a sound. The Judge turned towards the young girl.

'Annabil Stewart, in view of your youth and penitency, it has been decidit by the Lords of the Council that your life will be sparit. However, you will remain in the Prison House of Paisley for a period of ten years. Youthful ignorance, however, cannot be pleadit for the rest of you. In attempting to take away the life of another by sorcery, you deserve the severest penalty this court can award. On Monday next, therefore, the twenty-fourth of February in the year of our Lord, sixteen hundred and seventy-seven, Jonit Mathie Stewart, John Stewart, Bessie Weir, Margery Craige and Margaret Jackson, you will be condemmit to the fire to be burned and your effigies with you. May the Lord have mercy on your souls.'

Part Two

Doubt

Chapter Eleven

Nightmares

The sound of crackling wood and the feeling of falling, falling into the flames, her agonised body twitching and burning, brought Margaret into immediate wakefulness. She lay panting with relief, her heart racing. Almost a week had passed since the execution of the five accused of the bewitching of her father, and every night Margaret had been wakened by the same terrible visions. She rose from the bed, pulling a robe round her, crossed to the hearth and sat on the heavy oak chair in the light of the dying embers, shivering with cold and fear.

Her mother had remarked, only the day before, that the girl was looking pale and exhausted. When Margaret told her the nature of her nightmares, Lady Maxwell had been less than sympathetic. Her parents had urged her not to attend the executions. Her father warned that these gatherings were full of cut-purses, whores and the dregs of humanity, yet Margaret had not found that to be exactly true. Many of the ordinary citizenry of Paisley had attended. In atmosphere, the merriment and excitement was reminiscent of the Glasgow Fair, yet the outcome, the death and destruction of five human beings, was unimaginable in its brutality. What did you expect? Her brother John had asked. She did not know, indeed, had not thought it through. She had, perhaps, anticipated some kind of last minute reprieve, particularly for Jenny Mathie, who shouted her innocence even as the flames seared and scorched her ankles. What Margaret did not expect was the near carnival atmosphere. How had society become so brutalized, so inured to the suffering of others?

Although not a fanciful person she found the flickering shadows in her bedchamber not conducive to a return to sleep. Closing her eyes brought the same disturbing dreams. She decided to read in an effort to dispel the fearful images from her mind. She lit the candle on her bedside table and carried it over to the hearth, opened her cabinet and removed a shiny new book, one of the gifts her mother had brought from London. Margaret loved books, their feel, their smell. As a child attending the birthday parties of young relatives, Margaret would rarely join in the childish games. She would be found curled up amongst the presents, having extracted the expensive but carelessly discarded books from amongst their wrapping, trying desperately to read as many of them as she could before the carriage arrived to take her home. Lady Maxwell had expected her daughter to be ecstatic over the suit of clothes purchased from London's finest linen merchant, but Margaret's real joy was in the copy of Mr Shakespeare's *Macbeth*. Her mother's words, as she handed it over, 'I thought you would relish the Scottish connection,' were an understatement. Margaret loved Will Shakespeare's plays, every line a treasure trove to be mined for its abundance of verbal riches. This was deserving of two candles. She brought another over to the hearth and opened the book, read the list of *dramatis personae* and gave herself over to the joy of discovery, only to be stopped short by Shakespeare's opening scene, the entrance of three witches. She read it again. *Fair is foul and foul is fair, hover through the fog and filthy air.* She read the next scene and was dismayed to find that these foul creatures reappeared, boasting of their demonic powers. What was she to make of this? That someone as profound and well educated as William Shakespeare, believed in the power of witches? Or was he merely reflecting the beliefs of society. Was that not a playwright's purpose? To amplify common experience. To transform the ordinary into the extraordinary. Kings, Archbishops, scholars, and now perhaps Shakespeare himself believed in demonic power. But why should she feel so surprised, self-righteous even? Janet Douglas had easily convinced her that her father had been bewitched. What right had she to question now?

115

And yet she could not prevent herself from doing so. The nagging doubts, raised in her mind at the trial of those now convicted and executed at Paisley for witchcraft, refused to go away. She returned to bed, blew out her candles and tossed restlessly for another hour before succumbing to an exhausted sleep.

Chapter Twelve

Disappearance

Margaret was awakened next morning with the sun streaming through the diamond paned windows. Its fierce light had filtered through the small gap she had left in the curtains round her bed. She opened them completely, savouring the sunshine. She loved her bedroom. Her mother had allowed her to choose her bed curtains and quilt on their last trip to Edinburgh. They had a favourite shop there. 'As good as London,' her father would often say, in a vain effort to curtail his wife's expensive shopping trips down South. The owners imported the latest in bed linen from France and Holland through the port of Leith. After much deliberation, Margaret had chosen pale green silk, with wild flowers embroidered on the counterpane. Her mother had raised an eyebrow at the exorbitant price, but when she saw the girl's delight, she said nothing. She had even agreed to matching cushions for the chairs.

Margaret rose from the bed and walked bare-foot across the floor, throwing open the shutters which made up the bottom half of the windows. When the sun hit her counterpane it seemed as if the outside had come inside. Nature had found a way, she mused, half expecting to see tendrils creeping over the windowsill. She was brought down to earth by the icy blast. It was a deceptive winter sun with no real warmth. She closed the shutters hastily, washed and dressed quickly and made her way downstairs.

It was early. The other family members were still in bed. She helped herself to milk and freshly baked rolls. The Housekeeper apologised, saying the mutton collops were not yet ready. Margaret shrugged. She was not fond of cooked meat in the morning. At most she took an egg, which Cook offered to make for her. She thanked them both but contented herself with milk and rolls, anxious to be about the business which had kept her awake for a great part of the night.

She made her way to the office of Robert Fraser, Master of the Household. He was busy writing in a large account book, but rose on her entrance, gazing through his spectacles owlishly, surprised to see her. 'I thought that was Miss Douglas,' he said. 'May I help you Mistress?'

'It was Janet I wished to see.'

'She's aye down here by now. Will I send one o' the servants up to bring her doon? She's maybe owerslept.'

'I will go up myself. I wish a word with her,' said Margaret.

She preferred to question Janet without someone else present.

The girl had a reticence that was difficult to penetrate. Perhaps it would be easier to speak to her alone. She made for the stairs, climbed three flights, until she reached the little attic bedroom to which Janet had been assigned. Sir George felt that, as the girl seemed a different breed from the other servants, belonging to a somewhat higher social order, she should be in her own quarters, a fact that had caused a great deal of resentment amongst the staff. Margaret took a deep breath. During her sleepless hours she had planned the questions she wished to put to Janet. She was unsure of the reception she would be given. There was no denying the girl made her uneasy. She tapped on the door and waited. She could hear no stirring from within the room. She knocked on the door again and called out, waiting a few moments before cautiously turning the handle.

The room was empty. The bed looked as if no-one had slept in it. The hanging space was bare. The large kist at the bottom of the bed lay open. It contained pillows, but nothing belonging to Janet. There was nothing to show that she had ever occupied the room. Margaret hurried downstairs, passing Lizzie, one of the chambermaids. 'Have you seen Janet Douglas this morning?' Margaret asked.

'No, Mistress. Is she no' down workin' with Mr Fraser?'

Margaret shook her head. 'When did you last see her?'

'At supper last night.'

'Did she say anything about her plans for today?'

'No, Mistress', said Lizzie, a trifle sniffily, 'but then she disna talk much to the likes o' us.'

'There is nothing in her room,' said Margaret. 'She seems to have clearit oot.'

'She had a big brown bag wi' a' her stuff in it. I ken that for I cairrit it up the stairs,' said Lizzie, with more than a hint of resentment. 'Is that awa?'

'I saw no sign of it,' Margaret answered.

Robert Fraser could throw no light on Janet Douglas's disappearance either. She had given him no indication of her imminent departure. They came to the conclusion that she had left the house under cover of darkness. She had been living in Polloktoun prior to moving into Sir George's household, Robert informed her, but apart from that, he knew nothing. Even that piece of information surprised Margaret. She presumed the girl had been living in Glasgow. Had not Mary Robertson said as much, that she had 'taken her in'? When did she start living in Polloktoun? If she lived there, how did she travel to the Glasgow Fair to perform her act? There were a lot of unanswered questions. She asked Robert what he made of her.

'A richt hard worker,' he said, showing Margaret accounts written in Janet's neat handwriting. 'A lass o' few words. Didna' waste time bletherin'. That suited me.'

Chapter Thirteen

The Conversation

Margaret entered her father's bedchamber. Sir George was propped up in bed half-heartedly attempting to deal with some of his paperwork. A fire burned merrily in the grate. She was concerned at seeing his grey pallor, the dark circles under his eyes. He put aside his papers willingly. Margaret was always a welcome distraction. She had a keen enquiring mind. Their discussions usually had a much wider scope than those he had with his wife, beloved as Lady Maxwell was to him. He was surprised to hear of Janet's sudden departure. Margaret did not dwell on it, however. She felt he was troubled enough.

'You look tired Father. Did the pains keep you awake?' Margaret asked worriedly.

'No, no.' He always made light of his illness, as if denial would somehow alleviate his symptoms. ''Twas the damn foxes, howling awa' beneath my window.'

'It is the vixens, according to the gardener,' said Margaret. 'They aye return to where they were born to have their cubs.'

'Does it have to be beneath my window?' Sir George said testily.

'There is a hole in the bushes where they adjoin the house,' Margaret replied. 'Mother could ask Malcolm to block it up.'

'Set traps more like!'

'Oh, please dinna kill them,' Margaret said heatedly. 'There has been enough killing around here.'

He looked at her keenly. 'Are you still troubled wi' your nightmares?'

'I wish I had never gone to the executions,' said Margaret fervently. 'Jennie Mathie's cries haunt me yet.'

'I must confess that I had a greater belief in Scottish justice,' Sir George said gravely. 'I did not expect Jenny Mathie, or any of the others, to be put to the torch. My greatest regret is that my health kept me from championing their cause and putting the case for clemency.'

'I doubt that your intervention would have helpit,' said Margaret. 'Witchcraft trials seem to prey on folk's worst fears. Only the destruction of the accused appears to satisfy those involvit.'

'I too have been guilty of the same fanaticism in the past towards those sorry creatures.' There was true regret in her father's voice. 'Only the wisdom that comes wi' age has made me think again on it.'

'Dinna berate yoursel',' said Margaret, glancing down at the copy of *Macbeth* on her lap, 'even Mr Shakespeare seemed to believe in their satanic powers.'

'Or did he?' Sir George posed cynically. 'Patronage aye has a price.'

'You think their inclusion was to flatter the King?' mused Margaret. 'I have heard that said.'

'Perhaps, but the fellow was subtler than that,' replied Sir George.

'Perhaps he shows the dangers of self-fulfilling prophecy?' Margaret suggested.

'Jamie the Saxt was like a terrier,' her father opined. 'Once he had a rag atween his teeth he widna let go. His Majesty attended a number o' witchcraft trials when he was o'er in Denmark coortin' his wife. When his boat hit a storm on the way back, he blamit witchcraft for it.'

'You remember all this?' Margaret was fascinated.

'No, no. I was but a bairn when he died, but the country was full o' talk for years afterwards. His Majesty was not the only one wi' Scottish friends at court. Those he sent back so unceremoniously were more free wi' their tongues than perhaps discretion should allow.' He smiled. 'Rejection's aye been a bitter pill to swallow.'

'You think they exaggerated?' Margaret asked, intrigued.

'I doubt it. According to my father, if there were classes in manipulation, the King would hae been an excellent tutor. He was convincit he was God's anointed. He considered witchcraft not merely sacrilegious, but an act of treason. You should read his book on the subject. It is in my library.'

'You have a copy of *Daemonologie*?' Margaret asked, surprised.

'I do.'

'Why have I never seen it?'

''Tis in the top shelf o' the large bookcase. The one I keep lockit. I had nae wish to pit the fear o' death into you or your brothers and sisters. 'Tis nae exactly bedtime reading for bairns. You'll find the key in the library desk. But I warn you, it is no' easy reading.'

Margaret was never deterred at the thought of a challenge. He could see from her animated face that she relished it.

'There is another book on the same shelf which gives an alternative view, by Reginald Scot, 'The Discoverie of Witchcraft.' Worth having a look at, if only to restore some sense o' balance.'

'I look forward to reading them,' said Margaret rising. 'Meanwhile, Father, you should be resting. Not busying yourself with paperwork.'

'Decisions still have to be made, lass. The household does not run itsel'.' He rubbed his hand across his brow wearily. 'I hae just decidit to confine our carriage to the bonfire.'

'Why?' Margaret was dismayed at the thought of being confined to the limitations of the Pollok Estates.

'All these are bills,' her father said, indicating the pile of papers on his counterpane. 'I hae given a great deal o' money to the wheelwright. Oor roads take such a heavy toll. The Master Carpenter has already replaced the bodywork, but feels it needs done again. Like myself, it has reachit the end o' its usefulness.'

'Dinna talk like that Father,' said Margaret, distressed.

'I hae to be honest, my dear. I am merely saying I am like the carriage, getting old. Life has taken its toll. The Doctors do their best to patch up my old frame, but eventually I, too, will hae outlivit my natural span.'

Margaret's eyes brimmed with tears. She had rarely heard her father talk like this. He was usually such an optimistic man. He always kept up the pretence of feeling better in front of her mother. He knew Margaret was made of stronger stuff. Perhaps that was why he was being so forthright. He put his hand over hers.

'Dinna be upset, Margaret. It comes to all of us. Illness occurs rather more frequently as you age. My kidneys have never been of the best quality.' He smiled. 'If someone could make me a new pair I'd pay them handsomely. My recent bouts are just a warning, nothing, I'm convincit, to do wi' witchcraft. The only thing that troubles my conscience is that the courts had not the good sense to see that and acquit.'

He closed his eyes wearily. She looked down at him,

barely able to bear the thought that she might lose him. He looked as if the effort of talking had exhausted him and appeared to be drifting into sleep. She lifted the papers from his counterpane, placed them on his writing bureau, gently pulled the bedclothes round him and tiptoed from the room.

Chapter Fourteen

Investigation

It was next day before Margaret could pursue her literary quest. Lady Maxwell had assigned her, temporarily, to assist Robert Fraser in the copying of accounts. He was missing the assistance of Janet Douglas, a view not shared by her Ladyship. Whilst grateful for the intervention of Janet in rooting out those who plotted against Sir George, she had not taken to the girl.

'Civil enough and hard working, but there was something about her. She never looked you in the eye,' she said. 'I didna like having her under my roof.'

Margaret had worked quickly, impatiently, anxious to be about her literary investigations.

Next morning, immediately after breakfast, she made her way to the library. She unlocked the door on the top shelf of the largest bookcase, lifted down the copy of *Daemonologie* and studied the picture of the monarch on the front. What kind of king was this man, James the Sixth of Scotland and First of England, who felt it necessary to produce a book on Witchcraft, knowing the considerable influence it would have on his subjects? Indeed, as was quoted on the frontispiece from 'Ecclesiastes', *Where the word of a king is, there is power.*

She opened the book, curiously. It appeared to be in the form of a dialogue, divided into three parts. A passage in the Preface, addressed to the Reader, caught her eye. The King was saying that he was moved by his conscience *to preasse therebye, so farre as I can the resolve the doubting harts of many; both that such assaults of Satan are most certainly practized, and that the instruments thereof, merits most severely to be punished; against the damnable opinions of two principally in our age, whereof the one called Scot, an Englishman, is not ashamed in publike print to deny, that there can be such a thing as witchcraft.*

It was the name Scot, which drew Margaret up. Was this not the name her father had mentioned? She raised herself on tiptoe and felt along the top shelf. There was another book lying flat on the ledge. She lifted it down carefully and looked at the title, 'The Discoverie of Witchcraft', by Reginald Scot, the very man who had aroused the King's ire for his opposing views. She brought both books over to the desk at the window and sat down to read.

As she read the King's words, she found herself angry at the sheer injustice of his sentiments. In putting forward his argument as to why there were more women than men involved in witchcraft; a factor of twenty to one, by the King's reckoning, it stated,

The reason is easie, for that as that sexe is frailer than man is, so it is easier to be intrapped in these grosse snares of the Devill, as was over well proved to be true, by the Serpents deceiving of Eve at the beginning.

So this was His Majesty's justification for the persecution of these poor wretches.

As she read on, she was struck by the resonances with the confessions, the words and alleged deeds of the so called Pollok witches; the witches' marks, their rejection of their baptism, the clay models being produced, Satan taking the form of their dead husband, as in the case of Margaret Jackson. It was as if the King had produced a text book, a demonic catechism for the guidance of their prosecutors. He even urged towards the end of the book:

The Prince Magistrate for further tryals, may continue the punishing of them such a certaine space as he thinks convenient.

Was this not a justification for torture? thought Margaret indignantly. It was his admonition to the Magistrates, on arrival at their final judgment, which she found particularly disturbing:

But in the end to spare the life and not to strike when God bids strike, and so feverlie punish in so odious a fault and treason against God, it is not only unlawful, but doubtless no lesse sinne in that Magistrate. . . . And so comparable to the sin of witchcraft itself.

So if a judge was to find them innocent, his crime would be as great as witchcraft, by the King's reckoning. Any judge reading this manuscript, believing in the Divine Right of Kings, had only one course of action. It was a disturbing read. She put it down with great distaste and picked up 'The Discoverie of Witchcraft', hoping for a more balanced view.

The library door opened and her father appeared, fully dressed, looking better than he had done for weeks. The drawn look of pain had gone from his face. She rose to hug him, delighted to see him so improved. He had enjoyed the best night's sleep, he informed her, awaking pain free and energised. She told him of her anger at King James's view on witchcraft and on women in particular.

'Dinna judge him ower harshly,' said Sir George. 'There are those who say, even in these enlightened times, that a boy baby is born with a soul, but a girl acquires one much later.'

Margaret sighed, about to make an angry retort at this further injustice, but her father continued, 'If you are angry at anyone, lass, blame your own sex. James was only echoing the sentiments o' Queen Elizabeth. It was her Act brought in the death penalty for all who practised witchcraft. I suppose, if blame is to be apportioned,' he mused, 'it is probably the Church, who were, perhaps, ower zealous in seeking out the anti-Christ. Society itsel' is guilty, tae, for it aye looks for a scape-goat on which to place responsibility for a' its ills.'

Margaret was not totally convinced. Her father had not been present at the trial in Paisley. It was as if the Prosecution had used James's treatise as guidance. Sir George picked up the copy of Reginald Scot's book. 'You ken King James had this book banned? The copies were consignit to the flames,' he smiled, 'but I managed to save this yin. Like yoursel', Scot questions the whole idea o' witchcraft. He'll maybe be more to your taste. I'll leave you to your reading.' He crossed to the door. 'What you hae to mind, Margaret, is that some o' the greatest minds in society believe in witchcraft. The King was only reinforcing their sentiments. For mysel', I dinna ken what to think.'

Chapter Fifteen

Scepticism

She heard the crack of a twig behind her and spun round in alarm. She had the feeling of not being alone, of being watched. Probably just a poacher, Margaret reassured herself. Rabbits, ducks, fish; they were all, literally, fair game. Times were hard. An exceptionally wet spring and summer the year before had played havoc with the crops. Some of those who lived near the Pollok estate had little enough to eat. Who could blame them? Born in different circumstances, she might do the same herself, if she had a family to feed. She walked through the reeds to the river bank, clutching her bag of breadcrumbs, remnants of her breakfast. The little ducklings seemed agitated today; swimming around in circles, bumping into one another, calling out pathetically. Their mother was nowhere to be seen. There was a cloth bag lying by the river. She glanced around before opening it. The bag contained snares. She was right. She had disturbed a poacher. He had probably caught the mother duck, leaving her brood in disarray. She threw the bread to them, but they swam off, alarmed, no doubt afraid they might meet the same fate as their mother.

She looked over the fields to Polloktoun, seeing smoke curling lazily from several chimneys. Was Janet Douglas back living there? Gavin, one of the gardeners, lived in the village. Perhaps he would know. She made her way through the trees to the formal gardens, near the house, where she knew he was working, her mind mulling over the words of Reginald Scot. His book, 'The Discoverie of Witchcraft,' written in 1584, had a very different view from King James.

Witchcraft and inchantment is the cloke of ignorance, was how he put it. He condemned the wide-spread use of torture in obtaining confessions, saying the Pope himself would have renounced the Trinity and worshipped the devil upon his knees, had he been racked and tortured. He posed the obvious, but nonetheless, interesting question, that if witches had the power to cause illness, bring about the death of other people, why didn't they use it against their gaolers, torturers and Magistrates?

Margaret remembered the accusation, regarded as proof positive, against Jenny Mathie, that she had moved the stocks six yards, in order to obtain a bolster for her head. If she had the power that witches were supposed to exercise, why did she not destroy her gaolers and fly away on her broomstick? The ludicrous nature of the accusations and powers attributed to these poor wretches struck Margaret very forcibly. And all on the word of a comparative stranger. Margaret could do nothing to bring back her poor victims but perhaps she could clear their reputations and put a stop to any further malevolence at the hands of Janet Douglas.

She could see Gavin on his knees planting at the far end of the garden. She disliked the formality of this area. The rows of plants in their neat ranks seemed to her almost anti-Nature. Her mother, however, who took a great interest in gardening, had brought a variety of seeds back from London where formal gardens in the grounds of stately homes were increasingly popular. Lady Maxwell was most anxious that Scotland was not considered to be a poor relation in any sense, horticulturally or otherwise, hence the newly planted serried rows. She was deaf to her daughter's plea that Nature should not be constrained and fettered in this way. Margaret greatly preferred the woods, a haze of bluebells glimpsed through the trees, untamed, wild. She marvelled at the persistence of crocus amidst stones, grass and tree roots, all obstacles overcome, their biological imperative creating brush tips of yellow and purple. Defiant. Heartbreaking!

'When you are Mistress of your own house, Margaret,

you may do as you please,' were Lady Maxwell's final words on the matter.

Gavin looked up as Margaret approached, tipping his cap. He was fond of the girl, having known her since she was a child. She used to hunker down beside him, watching him plant, marvelling at the way he seemed to coax flowers to grow. If her childish offers of help hindered his work, he never showed any hint of irritation. A man of infinite patience, he went about his daily chores with an unhurried sense of calm. Having a conversation with him, however, was never easy. He spoke readily enough, but his words were always difficult to comprehend. She had, on many occasions, tried to work out what was wrong with his speech. As a child she had thought hairs from his thick black beard, now flecked with grey, were growing inside as well as outside his mouth, muffling his words, like her cat before it had coughed up a furball. It wasn't merely his rough accent, but that he appeared to have difficulty controlling his tongue. All too often, it poked through his teeth. His resultant lisp was a profound impediment to comprehension. Why was that? she had often asked herself. Surely we learn our speech from parents and family? Margaret wondered if Gavin's parents were similarly impaired. Did they have uncontrolled tongues? She had to fight the urge to push her fingertips against his tongue, forcing it behind his teeth, in order that he could hear the difference. If you were communing with plants and flowers all day, perhaps you did not feel the need to be understood.

She asked Gavin if he knew where Janet Douglas was living. A frown crossed his weather-beaten face. She had been lodging briefly in Polloktoun with Bessie Weir, one of the poor women who had been executed, he informed her. This, again, was a link that had not been brought up at the trial. Bessie's husband had put Janet out of the house when Jenny Mathie was arrested.

'Threw her bits and pieces intae the gutter,' he said, with a certain satisfaction. 'But there were others who would hae taken her in. Them that thocht she was the saviour o' your faither. If she's left the castle for good, perhaps she's gone back to Polloktoun.'

'What did you think of her?' asked Margaret.

'I took naethin' to dae wi' her,' the man replied. He returned to his planting, a trifle dismissively, but as she made to walk away, he called after her.

'Hae a word wi' Charlie Evans. He could tell you a tale or twa.'

Chapter Sixteen

Polloktoun

The mare picked her way carefully over the ford. She was a sure footed, docile creature. Margaret, though not the best of horsewomen, had no misgivings when she was on Nellie's back. The animal scrambled up the bank. With a gentle pull on the reins, Margaret pointed her in the direction of Polloktoun. It was a grey forbidding morning. The mist hanging eerily over the river seemed to silence the birds, but it was a short journey and Margaret did not have the patience to wait for a better day. At this time of the year, to be free of rain or snow was good enough weather in which to ride out.

The village sat on the southern banks of the White Cart river, positioned to intercept the main Paisley to Glasgow road. Not that many travellers stopped there. There was no welcoming tavern. Set amongst rolling farmland, its main interest was its association with a Mediaeval Charter, the land of Nether Pollok being part of a land grant scheme from Walter Fitz Allan, High Steward of Scotland, five hundred years earlier to one of his retainers, an Anglo-Norman knight by the name of de Polloc. Margaret's ancestors married into his family and the Maxwells became the primary landowners.

The village was no distance at all, yet Margaret could barely see it until she was about five yards away, when dark shapes suddenly loomed out of the mist. They revealed themselves to be stone buildings, simple single storey structures, with small plots of land on which the tenants could grow crops. Margaret had been in Polloktoun before, but never alone. As most of the villagers were employed in some capacity on the Pollok estate, she had accompanied her mother on some of her charitable excursions to visit sick or destitute tenants. She had intended accompanying her father to visit the Stewarts when Jenny Mathie's husband, the Under Miller died, but Nellie was lame that day and Sir George had gone alone to offer his condolences.

As the mare clopped along the dirt track road through the village she wondered if she would find Janet Douglas. Why had she left the castle in the middle of the night? Of what was she afraid? Margaret had a number of questions requiring answers. The main street was deserted, the houses shuttered, huddled against the cold. She suddenly caught a glimpse of a group of ragged little children playing with a ball in one of the alleys. Despite the bitter cold, they were barefoot and lightly clad. Their little faces were pinched, their noses red, but they seemed to be engrossed and enjoying their game, so much so that they seemed genuinely surprised when she turned her horse toward them and interrupted their play.

'I'm looking for Mr Evans, the carter,' said Margaret, smiling.

One of the two little girls, who looked like sisters, with the same reddish hair, bright blue eyes and startled expressions came forward. She seemed about to say something, but when she took in the rich dark green velvet of Margaret's riding outfit, she shrank back, as if trying to disappear into herself. She was not used to seeing grand ladies in Polloktoun. A slightly older boy with a green snotter, making a track like caterpillar slime down his grimy face, looked at Margaret curiously, before replying. 'Ower there.' He wiped his nose on his ragged sleeve and pointed. 'The hoose at the end.'

They watched curiously as she dismounted and tied her horse to a post, but seemed to lose interest as she approached Charlie Evans's door. The older boy started to bounce the ball rhythmically, before delivering a hard kick. The ball disappeared down the main street, swallowed up in the mist. They all ran off in pursuit, bored with the temporary diversion which the grand lady had provided.

Margaret hesitated, gathering her thoughts and mentally wording her enquiry, before gently tapping on the door. There was no response from inside. She waited a few moments, leant forward and rapped more vigorously. The door swung open under her weight, taking her by surprise and projecting her a few feet into the room. In the gloom she saw Charlie Evans asleep in a chair, near the fire which had all but gone out. He had a worn woollen blanket around him. The house was cold and, judging from the smell, seemed to be shared with livestock. She could hear the sound of a cow coming from over the rough partition wall. She coughed gently and, when that elicited no response, called his name. The man came to, with a start, surprised to see her standing there. He was tousled and unkempt with a few days growth of beard.

'Your door was unlockit, Mr Evans,' Margaret said, with a hint of apology for her intrusion.

'Nobody locks their door in Polloktoun.' He grimaced as he shifted his position. 'Forgive me for not getting up, Miss Margaret, but I seem to have broken my bloomin' leg.' He threw aside the blanket to reveal a crudely bandaged leg with a makeshift splint. 'Fell on the bliddy ice, forgive my language. Out the back there, digging up the winter kale. The feet just went away from me.'

Margaret knew that this spelled economic disaster for a man like Charlie Evans, who got paid only when he made deliveries. She resolved to say something to her father. She knew the man had a family to keep. Charlie was something of a rarity in Polloktoun, an Englishman, despite his Welsh name. Formerly a driver on the London to Glasgow coach, he had fallen for the barmaid at the Glasgow tavern which served as a coach stop. A red haired, blue-eyed beauty, she only agreed to marry him if they could stay near her family in the neighbouring village of Pollokshaws. Margaret realised why the two red haired blue-eyed girls she had seen outside, looked so familiar. They appeared cast from the same mould as his wife, whom Margaret had met when the woman appeared, on a weekly basis, in the Great Hall, delivering butter and eggs in lieu of rent. She had been one of the villagers who had called to enquire after the health of Sir George. Charlie explained that his wife was over in Pollokshaws helping one of the washerwomen. 'Only pays a few merks, but every little helps right now.' There was no self-pity in Charlie's voice. It was merely a statement of fact.

When Margaret explained the purpose of her visit and mentioned Janet Douglas, propriety kept Charlie from spitting at the name, but she could hear the contempt in his voice.

'Jenny Mathie was a good woman. Saved the life o' my wife when she delivered our two daughters. My Ellen was broken-hearted at her burnin'. The others were decent folk, too. Maybe Jenny's son was a bit o' a wild lad, I grant you, but then he was but sixteen. Hadn't yet learned sense, but he was no warlock.'

'Yet others from around here spoke out agin them at the trial,' said Margaret.

'The Mathie family were a bit better off,' said Charlie. 'Being Under Miller at Shawbridge Mill, Jennie's husband was allowed to keep a small amount of what they ground. Jealousy's a powerful emotion, particularly amongst folks who don't have much.'

'What do you know of Janet Douglas?' asked Margaret.

'Not a lot,' said Charlie. 'Should do, for I gave her a regular run in the cart to Glasgow, when she was doing her trickery at the Glasgow Fair.'

'You think her mind reading act was trickery?'

'According to my wife, Alan Geddes, the showman, was the biggest fraudster who ever walked the streets o' Glasgow. He'd been barred from the tavern where she worked because o' his tricks. He'd parted one too many of the regulars from their silver. If Janet Douglas worked for him at the Fair she must have been in on his act.'

'Did she ever talk to you about foretelling Father's illness?'

'She never talked, full stop, during our journeys. Acted as if she was a dumbie.'

'You think it was an act?'

'Well, what do you think, Mistress? She recovered her speech quick enough to accuse decent folks.'

'Do you think she knew who I was?'

'Everybody in Polloktoun knows who you are, Miss Margaret. We know all the Maxwells. We're dependent on your family for a living. She would need to be blind, as well as dumb, not to know you.'

So she probably recognised me that day at the Fair, thought Margaret. Living in Polloktoun, she would hear about Sir George's recurring illness. Her act was, indeed, beginning to smell of trickery.

She began to wonder if the fat man accused of adultery was in on the act. There had been a faint whiff of farce about the couple as he ran off, pursued by his irate wife.

'Can you think of any reason why Janet Douglas wished ill against Jenny Mathie Stewart?'

'Well,' he mused, 'Jenny refused to take her in when she knocked on her door looking for bed and board. The Stewarts have the biggest house in the village, but Jenny's daughter and family come on regular visits from Glasgow, so she needed the space.'

'A reasonable excuse.'

'I dunno. Maybe Janet Douglas did not see it that way,' Charlie said thoughtfully. 'There was no knowin' what went on in that lass's mind.'

'So Bessie Weir took her in?'

He nodded, a saddened expression on his face. 'Aye, God rest the poor woman.'

Margaret had a sudden image of Bessie's pathetic, life-less body burning alongside the others.

'Her poor man has been demented wi' grief since her death. He's taken the children and moved away to be with his folks in Hamilton.'

'They did say Bessie cursed my father for not employing her husband in the harvest,' Margaret said quietly.

'There's a great difference between speakin' ill and acting ill. We all moan about our employers. Does not mean we wish them any harm, Mistress.' He took his injured leg in his hands and moved it to a more comfortable position, gritting his teeth against the pain. 'Folk round here have a great deal of respect for Sir George. Many have Covenanting relatives who owe their life to him, if you catch my drift.'

Margaret felt slightly uncomfortable. That her father's trips to the hills were common knowledge, worried her. Prior to his illness, he had regularly left, ostensibly for a days riding, but, in reality, bringing supplies to those who held their secret conventicles in the open air. He even allowed them to hold illegal meetings in the Castle. He had, again, put himself in danger of imprisonment with his Covenanting sympathies. She thanked Charlie Evans for his time, wished him a speedy recovery and made to leave, but turned back at the door.

'Have you any idea where Janet Douglas is living now?'

'I heard from one o' the other carters that she was in Glasgow, but whereabouts I've no idea. I can tell you this though, Polloktoun is well rid o' her.'

As she pointed the mare in the direction of home, Margaret mulled over the facts she'd gleaned. Janet had lived in Polloktoun briefly, prior to Sir George's alleged bewitching. She would know her way about the village and who lived where. According to Charlie Evans no-one locked their door. Janet would have had ample opportunity to enter the homes of the accused and plant her clay images. Margaret still could not fathom any real reason for her behaving like this, but she was resolved that no-one else would fall victim to Janet Douglas's accusations.

Chapter Seventeen

The Prison Visit

Ewan looked at his wife worriedly. It seemed as if some-one had taken the fun-loving, garrulous and full of life Mary Robertson and replaced her with this pale, silent shadow of a woman. She was walking round the house, preoccupied, quietly removing food from the cupboard, wrapping it carefully in a clean cloth and placing it in her bag. He had seen her packing some clean clothes and hoped they would be given to their intended recipient. Stories abounded about corruption in Paisley prison; goods intended for prisoners being sold off. Mary returned Ewan's kiss, absentmindedly, as she left on her journey.

Charlie Evans usually climbed down from the cart to help

her up, but today he remained seated. Although he had declared himself fit for work, Charlie's leg was still giving him trouble. He was limping badly. It was obviously a more complicated break than he first realised and despite his wife's administrations, had not set properly. The leg bone was sticking out at a peculiar angle; putting weight on it caused a pain to shoot up into his hip. When he packed the heavy load of timber he was taking to Paisley, the leg kept giving way beneath him, but he merely stopped for a moment till the pain lessened, before stoically carrying on. Three months of near idleness had almost ruined him. There was another baby on the way. He had no choice but to work. Mary was always generous in giving him a handful of coins in payment for the journey, for which he was extremely grateful. She was unusually quiet today, but who could blame her? To lose three members of your family, in such horrific circumstances, was enough to drive anyone over the edge.

It was market day. There were three a week now in Glasgow but this one was mainly dedicated to food. The aroma of cooking assailed his nostrils. The stalls were doing a thriving business in goods like butter, herring, pig's trotters, salt and prunes. The Glasgow wifies were going from stall to stall, haggling for the best price, blocking the street at times, and making it difficult for Charlie to pass, drawing him baleful looks if he nudged the horse in their direction. Mary seemed indifferent to the sights and sounds of Glasgow life. A fellow sweetmeat seller called out and waved from her stance on the bridge, but Mary did not appear to hear her, or if she had, she did not acknowledge the greeting. Charlie glanced at the woman by his side, concerned. She seemed worried, distracted, as indeed, she was. The only time the poor woman felt a semblance of happiness was first thing in the morning, in that limbo between sleep and wakefulness, then she would remember. The feeling of letting her mother down threatened to overwhelm her. Her chest felt tight. Her heart raced. She had promised to visit Annabil in Paisley prison but, since her mother's execution, had only been once and even that had been three months earlier. Since Charlie's accident it had been almost impossible to obtain transport. The last time she had to do the journey in stages. The carter had been a lecher whose drink fuelled advances she had to fight off. If she had told Ewan, a quick tempered giant of a man, he would have killed him. She knew she was safe in the hands of Charlie Evans, one of the most decent men that walked the earth. They were soon clear of the main streets and passing the public green. Charlie wondered, idly, why there was no washing on display, but he heard cheers and saw a group of male runners tearing round the outskirts of the green. A foot race had been arranged and the crowd were on the sidelines shouting encouragement to their favourites. When he pointed it out to Mary she glanced over, but with no real interest. Her thoughts were on Annabil. The girl was more like a daughter to her than a sister. Mary had been a young married woman when her little sister was born. Jenny Mathie was quite ill after her painful confinement with Annabil. As she said herself. 'I'm nae spring chicken. Gey old to be havin' a bairn.'

Mary had moved into her mother's house and taken care of the baby until Jenny's strength returned. The thought of that child, for so she still considered Annabil, of her suffering in Paisley prison until she reached twenty four years of age, filled Mary with panic and gnawing guilt. Ewan was awakened night after night with the sound of his wife sobbing into the pillow. She would not be comforted. She told herself she could have made a greater effort to visit the girl, find another mode of transport. Truth be told, she was afraid. Since her meeting at Pollok, when Janet Douglas had declared that Mary, too, was a witch, she had lived in fear and dread of every knock on the front door. Reason told her that the witch's mark pointed out by Douglas, was nothing of the sort, merely a scar left when she fell from some rocks as a child, but others might not be convinced. Her mother, brother, aunt and two neighbours had died on Janet Douglas's testimony and her young sister languished in prison. She was terrified that she, too, might be apprehended when she appeared at the gaol. She had wrestled long and hard with her conscience. Duty had prevailed. Annabil was only a child. Mary must bring her succour and consolation. Her mother's memory demanded it.

When Charlie dropped her at Paisley prison gates after the morning's journey, he noticed she was trembling. Her face was ashen. He wished he could go with her for support, but it was impossible. The timber had to be delivered to a yard at the other end of Paisley. He gripped her hand firmly and promised to be waiting by the gates in an hour.

The inside of Paisley prison with its ragged, wretched inmates, hands reaching through the bars, calling out in distress, was like a vision of hell. As she waited nervously for Annabil to be brought to her in the stinking grey hole that seemed to serve as some kind of reception room, a young gaoler appeared, clutching a letter.

'You are next o' kin to Jonit Mathie Stewart and John Stewart. Are ye no'? Them that wis burnit?'

'Yes,' Mary answered faintly.

'This is for you.' He handed her the letter and left.

She unfolded it with trembling hands. Was this the summons she had been dreading? Was she to be arrested? It appeared to be an account. Across the top it read:

Costs for the execution of Jonit Mathie Stewart and John Stewart on 24th February 1677:

The items underneath swam before her eyes.

For twenty loads of coal to burn them	£4	2s	8d
For two tar barrells	£1	18s	
For tinders		14s	
To him that brought the executioner	£3		
To the executioner for his paines	£9	2s	
For his expenses here		18s	4d

The accompanying note stated that the account had to be paid by the next of kin five weeks from the date of receipt; otherwise a severe penalty would be exacted.

Mary was still reeling from the sheer insensitivity, the cruelty of the letter when Annabil was ushered in. She barely recognised the emaciated, ragged, filthy creature that stood before her. All bloom of youth had completely gone from Annabil's face. Her jaws were sunken, her eyes dull and lifeless. When the Turnkey locked the door behind him, leaving them alone, the girl threw herself into Mary's arms, sobbing. 'I knew you wid come. I knew you wid tak' me home.'

Mary was stricken. How could she tell the girl that she had another nine and a half years still to serve in this hellish place? Instead, she brought out the bag containing food. The Turnkey had attempted to take it from her earlier but she had quickly slipped him a bribe. He had glanced at the money in his hand, transferred it swiftly into his pocket, like a sleight of hand, before removing the clothes.

'She'll hae those later, when she's had a wash,' he said.

Mary doubted if Annabil would ever see them. Judging from the rags she was wearing, he must have sold the last lot. The young girl took the food from her, ran into a corner and ate ravenously, glancing around quickly, like an animal, as if it was going to be taken from her.

When she had finished all but a piece of bread, which she concealed in the pocket of her ragged dress, she suddenly looked up and fixed Mary with an accusatory stare.

'You're not taking me home,' she said. 'Are you?'

Mary shook her head, fighting back her tears, 'I cannot sweetheart. The courts winna let me.'

The girl began to weep. Mary threw her arms round her, hugging her to her breast.

'I hate it here. Those men dae bad things to me,' Annabil sobbed. 'Terrible things! They hurt me.'

Mary could think of nothing to say by way of consolation. She clung to the girl, her own tears falling on top of Annibil's matted hair.

The door was suddenly unlocked. The Turnkey stood there, jangling his keys. 'Time's up,' he said.

Mary stood up reluctantly, Annabil still clinging to her. He crossed over quickly. 'None o' that, now.' He removed Annabil's tight grip from her sister's cloak. 'Visiting's over.'

Mary turned away in distress and made for the door. She was stopped by Annabil's anguished cry. 'Tell Mother it wisna my fault. They made me say those things. Please tell her.'

Chapter Eighteen

The Suicide

Sir George lay back against the plush red upholstery. With the steady motion of the new carriage, he felt his eyes closing. When his wife had first witnessed his purchase she felt it a trifle ostentatious, with its gilt and burgundy façade, but she had said nothing, not wishing to dampen her husband's delight and enthusiasm. Sir George's reason for buying the best he could afford was not for show, but for comfort. He was feeling the benefit of its superior springing as it journeyed towards the town of Glasgow. It was commodious, too. His wife, daughters Annabelle, Margaret and son Zacharias were all comfortably seated and did not appear to be too crowded.

News of the baby's birth had been greeted with sheer

delight in the Maxwell household. His eldest daughter, Marian and her husband James had been trying to conceive for three years and had all but given up hope when their son was born. The birth of a little grandson seemed to re-energise Sir George. He had been spending a great deal of his time in bed. 1677 had been a bad year for him. His recurring ill health had worn him down, not just in body, but in spirit. A depression appeared to have come over him. He hated that illness seemed to define him and rule the quality of his life. What was it Master Shakespeare had said? Something about the Lord 'turning his canon 'gainst self-slaughter.' If it were not for his religious convictions and the thought of leaving his beloved wife and family he might have refused Doctor Bremner's medications and speeded his own departure. Little Archibald's birth had changed all that. Sir George's delight in the news almost overwhelmed him. Tears of happiness had coursed down his cheeks. What was that about, he wondered? The idea of continuance perhaps? For whatever reason, he felt himself in better spirits than he had for months and had arranged this family outing to Glasgow to see his little grandson at the first opportunity.

Margaret looked across at her father. His eyes were still closed, so thankfully could not see her worried look. Although the birth of the baby had given him a boost, she knew that he was a very sick man. When she mentioned her concern to Lady Maxwell, her mother appeared not to agree. Margaret felt this was self-deception on her mother's part. Her Ladyship's way of dealing with bad news was to pretend it did not exist. If you do not give it credence, it will go away, seemed to be her unspoken motto.

The coach suddenly drew to a standstill, interrupting Margaret's thoughts and awakening her father, who was thrown slightly forward, but saved from accident by his wife's restraining arm. Margaret looked out of the window. They were approaching the Brig o' Clyd near the Stockwell straits, but the way ahead appeared blocked. People were milling about, talking excitedly to one another. Many were peering over the parapet, while others jostled for a place in order to do the same. Sir George stuck his head out of the window. 'What is the matter?'

'Somebody's jumpit aff the Brig, sir. Killt hersel',' said the coachman.

The incident dampened the spirits of the family for the remainder of the journey but, by unspoken agreement, they hid this from their hosts, Marian and James, and did not let it affect their delight in meeting little Archibald, who was passed around like a parcel. Margaret held the baby to her, loving his softness and his baby smell. Despite her avowed intention to remain unmarried until she had made her mark on the world, when he gripped her finger she hugged him to her, feeling something akin to a maternal urge that took her totally by surprise. As she gazed down at his innocent little face, she had a sudden vision of ash flying on to his cheek and shuddered at the recollection. Would she ever be free of those horrifying images?

It was not until evening, over a wonderful dinner of chicken and venison and a table groaning with culinary delights, that the subject of the suicide on the bridge was raised. The elder Maxwell son, John, had joined them for dinner. He had now joined a busy law practice in Glasgow and found that due to work commitments he was able to join in family occasions far less than he would have liked. He had made a special effort to be there that night and was regaling the company with hilarious tales from the law courts. His young brother, Zacharias, who had listened to the adult conversation in bored silence, suddenly piped up,

'Did you ken a lady jumpit off the bridge and killt hersel? We saw it when we were comin' here,' he said importantly.

John nodded gravely. Yes, he knew about it. Marian and her husband wanted to hear all the details. They had been so bound up in their new arrival for the past two weeks that they were unaware of what was going on in the outside world. John cast a sidelong look at his father before speaking.

'Her name was Mary Robertson. She was a sweetmeat seller in the town.'

Margaret gasped. 'Jenny Mathie's daughter?'

'Apparently,' said John, 'she had been suffering black humours since her family were burnit at the stake.'

'She foretelt it,' said Margaret, barely able to control her mixture of excitement and unease. 'Janet Douglas said that she would drown in the river.'

'That woman's name aye comes up,' said John. 'She,

herself, is now the subject of investigation. Your friend, Professor Sinclair, has again written to me about her.'

'She accusit Mary Robertson o' being a witch. The puir woman was terrified,' said Sir George, thinking back to the night Janet Douglas had torn the collar from Mary's dress to expose a so-called witch's mark.

'Do you ken where Janet Douglas is?' asked Margaret.

'She's been working in the candle-factory, causing mayhem, from what I hear,' John replied.

'In what way?' asked Sir George.

'She accusit yin o' the workers there, an auld wifie that never did ony harm to onybody, o' being a witch. The puir auld sowel has lost her wits, apparently. Disnae ken her ain family ony mair.'

'Janet Douglas needs to be stoppit,' said Sir George.

'I'm beginning to wonder from whence her powers are coming,' mused John. 'Perhaps they burnit the wrong yins at the stake.'

'But those folk confessit,' said Lady Maxwell, confused.

'They were tortured,' said Margaret. 'They would hae confessit to onything.'

'We do not know that,' her father cautioned.

'Tell him, John,' Margaret spoke angrily. 'We call oorsel's a civilised society, yet we extract confessions using the rack, thumbscrews, the brack, onything to obtain a conviction.'

'This is hardly dinner table conversation,' Lady Maxwell admonished.

'Tell them, John. It is true, is it not?' Margaret said, a

flush on her cheeks. 'You represent the law. You ken what goes on.'

'Well, the authorities do consider that, in some cases, the end justifies the means,' John admitted quietly.

Chapter Nineteen

The Great Fire of Glasgow

November 1677

Janet Douglas woke up with the acrid smell of burning in her nostrils. Her fellow prisoners were coughing, trying desperately to raise themselves up from their straw mattresses as smoke poured through the bars of the cell door, threatening to overcome them.

Her lungs felt as if they were on fire. With a supreme effort, she dragged herself to the door and began pounding on it. Three of the others crawled over and joined in, shouting with what was left of their lung power for help. The fifth occupant, an old, frail woman had already succumbed to the smoke and was lying still and lifeless. Just when they had assumed that their gaolers had flown, there was a sound of coughing from outside the door. They renewed their shouts. A key turned in the lock. 'Quick, get oot o' here,' a burly man stood there. 'The toon's ablaze! We've broke the door doon.'

The ground floor was on fire. Somehow, Janet made it down the stairs; following the man they desperately battled their way through the flames, wooden beams crashing around them. She did not look back to see if the others had made it. Miraculously, only her hair and eyebrows were scorched. Outside all was confusion. A Glasgow mob had indeed broken down the door of the Tollbooth in order to free the prisoners. They were incensed that the gaolers had left the inmates, many of whom were Covenanters, to perish in the flames. The night sky was red and angry. The whole of Glasgow seemed to be alight. People were running in all directions, some carrying pails of water in a futile attempt to save their homes, their possessions, their families.

One hundred and thirty wooden and thatch homes were destroyed that night and many of the town's inhabitants lost their lives. The fire had been started deliberately in a blacksmith's shop by a disgruntled apprentice in revenge for a beating from his master. But none of this was of interest to Janet Douglas. She quickly detached herself from the small group of prisoners foolishly milling about outside the burning prison and joined those who were making their escape. They ran in a group, not quite knowing where they were going, constantly finding their way blocked by flames. Janet soon separated from them and by plunging down one alley and then another, found herself close to the river where some of the townspeople had formed a human chain, passing buckets of water in a vain attempt to quench the thirst of the angry flames. Others were using long hooked poles to remove the burning thatch from their houses. She ran past them with only one intention, to escape from this town. It would only be a matter of time before the prisoners would be rounded up. She made her way to the house where she had been staying. It was empty. Her fellow tenants had obviously taken flight, aware that the flames were heading in their direction. She lifted a floorboard where she had hidden some money, hastily threw a few items of clothing into a bag and quickly left, running as fast as she could to put some distance between herself and the town.

Chapter Twenty

Demise

Doctor William Bremner was awakened from a deep sleep. This time it was not his wife's snoring which had disturbed him, but her large, rotund figure standing over him, shaking him mercilessly until he opened his bleary eyes.

'There is somebody at the door, William,' she said.

This time he heard the pounding for himself. He glanced at the clock over on the mantelpiece. Four a.m. He swung his legs wearily out of the bed and shuffled over to the window to see who was inconsiderate enough to call at this hour. Recognising Sir George Maxwell's coach and the liveried coachman, he drew his robe quickly around himself and hurried downstairs.

Laurence Martin, Sir George's servant stood there. The man seemed very distressed. 'Sir George is awfu' sick,' he said. 'Come quick, sir!'

The doctor dressed hastily, grabbed his bag and made his way out to the carriage, glancing up at the distant sky, curiously. There seemed to be a strange red glow in the direction of Glasgow.

Laurence Martin held open the carriage door and helped him in. Doctor Bremner had no sooner parked his bottom on the seating than they were off, heading at a fast pace towards the castle at Pollok.

They need not have hurried, thought the good Doctor as he entered Sir George's bedroom. Surrounded by his family, Sir George lay, propped up on pillows, his breathing pattern one that Doctor Bremner had witnessed many times during a lifetime attending to the dying. Sir George was clearly beyond any help that he could administer. The doctor's presence, however, seemed to give Lady Maxwell comfort in the last hour of her husband's life; an assurance that everything was being done for Sir George that could be done, as he gradually and peacefully slipped away.

Part Three

Retribution

Chapter Twenty-One

Canongate Prison, Edinburgh

Sixteen months later

The young woman who, for a long time, had been the object of Margaret Maxwell's deliberations and those of the late Sir George was, at that moment, enduring the life of a wretched creature. Indeed Reginald Scot's words from 'The Discoverie of Witchcraft' seemed extremely apposite in the case of Janet Douglas. Why would anyone with magical, satanic powers at their disposal allow themselves the indignity and suffering of incarceration in a dark, damp, filthy cell in Edinburgh's Canongate Prison? The crime for which she was presently imprisoned was the one which, largely due to her allegations, five people burned at the stake in Paisley. Ironically, the accuser was now the accused. The crime of Malicious Mischief, for which she was sentenced nine months earlier, causing her to be *stripped nakit from the waist upward, fastened to a cart's airse and whipped through the streets of Edinburgh until she be bloodie* now seemed mild in comparison. She had shut the memory of that day from her mind, refusing to dwell on the indignity and pain. The fact that she did not react to the Edinburgh mob who jeered and spat at her as she was scourged at the street corners, seemed to urge them on to further humiliations. It had been a market day and the streets were mobbed. Being Saturday, many of the onlookers were fuelled by alcohol. As she staggered painfully after the piper heading the procession of rabble rousers, who added to the cacophony by beating tin plates, or anything they could lay their hands on, rotten fruit and vegetables rained down upon her. This was followed by shovelfuls of foul smelling dung and the equally pungent contents of chamber pots. Janet Douglas's reputation had gone before her.

Now, however, the charge was much more serious. A number of Scottish worthies, including a local Edinburgh goldsmith and his family and a leading Glasgow minister of some repute, had been outraged when she escaped from Glasgow and was released after her first charge in Edinburgh, following, what seemed to them to be, minor punishments. Her accusations of witchcraft, against them and many others of unimpeachable reputation, had caused uneasy mutterings amongst the populace of Edinburgh. This time they grew to a ground swell. It was no longer considered malicious mischief that Janet Douglas was practising, but something much darker. To constantly harp on the work of Satan, as she did, led many to believe that she, herself, was in his thrall. On the eleventh March 1679 a charge of *having had a familiar and consulting evil spirits* was laid against Janet Douglas at her trial by the Privy Council in Edinburgh. No specific demonic details were given in the charge. It was hoped that these could be obtained in the process of her trial. A conclusion of witchcraft would be a satisfactory one for all. For almost two years she had been a thorn in the flesh of the Scottish authorities with her accusations. Details of her part in the so called 'bewitching of Sir George Maxwell' were familiar to many of the Privy Council Members, as indeed the man himself had been, serving, as he did, with some of them in the Scottish Parliament as a young man. His death, sixteen months earlier, from what appeared to be a recurring kidney complaint, led many to cast doubts on the charge of 'bewitching,' that had been laid against his unfortunate tenants. A feeling that the wrong people had been burned at the stake was beginning to gather momentum.

Chapter Twenty-Two

Fellow Prisoner

She was interrupted from a sound and dreamless sleep. Most of the prisoners found it impossible to sleep properly in the filth and putrid stench of the Canongate prison, but not Janet. Those sharing her cell and anchored to the floor by chains beside her, found her a puzzle. She seemed to take everything in her stride. Even when her request for lighter shackles was refused, she accepted the decision with equanimity. Others had purchased them. They gave some measure of relief from the chafing and cuts caused by the heavier ones. Provided you had money to pay for them they were usually available, but the gaoler had spat on the filthy floor in front of her, refusing her proffered merks, saying, 'They're no' for witches.'

A shaft of light from a lantern lit up the gloom. 'Janet Douglas, come wi' me.' She rubbed the sleep from her eyes and blinking in the half light, rose from her straw bed. James Meikle, a fair haired youth chained next to Janet, awoke to see the shining bald head of the gaoler jerk in the direction of the heavy wooden door. Janet disappeared through it and the key turned in the lock, plunging her cellmates back into the gloom.

'Do you think she's awa' to be burnit?' The hoarse croaky voice came from a dark corner, where a ragged, toothless old vagrant called Meg, was chained.

'She's no' been sentenced yet. They've nae proof of witchcraft,' James replied. He found it hard to believe that someone seemingly as young as Janet could be involved in the black arts. He had asked her age, to which she'd replied, 'What age do you thing I am?'

She had an annoying habit of turning a question into another question whenever she spoke, which was very rarely. Others told of their lives almost as a way of passing the time, or proclaiming their innocence. James was honest, inasmuch as he admitted to being a felon, imprisoned for a first offence. He had taken a gold watch from a drunk outside a tavern, urged on by the bad company he had fallen into and the amount of ale he, himself, had consumed.

He guessed Janet was about fourteen or fifteen but was unsure, as her demeanour seemed more composed, older.

In fact she did not know what age she was. She reckoned about seventeen or eighteen, but being slim and slight, with almost a boyish figure she could easily pass for younger. It suited her to do so.

Chapter Twenty-Three

Interrogation

George Hickes shivered in the dank, damp atmosphere of the Chief Gaoler's office, removed a lace edged handkerchief from his person and blew his nose with a trumpeting sound. He had awakened that morning with the feeling of having swallowed broken glass. His throat felt on fire. When Bessie, his servant girl, had brought breakfast, he left it untouched, an unusual occurrence. He was very fond of his food as the pillow of fat around his middle testified. Today, however, the act of swallowing felt almost impossible. His physician had told him to gargle with warm salt water, which he had done at regular intervals. 'Ideally,' the doctor said 'you should stay in bed.' He knew this was sound advice but he had waited too long for a meeting with Janet Douglas to risk cancelling. It had taken him almost a year to arrange this appointment. Another opportunity to converse with this intriguing girl might not be forthcoming.

It was not mere curiosity that drove him. George Hickes was a cleric, but no ordinary one. Domestic chaplain to the Duke of Lauderdale, High Commissioner to Scotland, Hickes numbered Samuel Pepys, Dr Burnet, Archbishop of Glasgow, and Dr Rosse, Lord Bishop of Argyle, amongst his friends. Indeed it was the latter gentleman who had arranged this meeting, despite an order from the Privy Council that no one should be admitted to Janet Douglas, a ruling which the Lord Bishop had managed to override. Whilst unwilling to prejudice her case in any way, the Privy Council were as anxious as anyone else to throw some light on the nature of the young girl's power. It was widely known that George Hickes had contributed scholarly essays on the phenomenon of Second Sight. In his opinion, it was unclear whether events, apparently 'revealed' by those individuals, stemmed from a good or evil cause. The Council were aware of an absence of proof in the charges against Janet Douglas. Any details that could be elicited would be welcome. To that end, they insisted on the presence of a witness at the meeting, the Reverend Mr Scott, Minister of the Church of the Abbey of Holyrood.

The two men rose as Janet Douglas was ushered through the doorway. Her shackles had been removed and she strode into the room as though she owned it. The gaoler closed the door and stood against it, his arms folded.

'You may leave us,' said Hickes to the man, dismissively.

'I'll bide here. The lass is my responsibility.' His tone ruled out any argument. Hickes exchanged a look with the Reverend Scott, who shrugged his acceptance. To be honest, Scott was grateful for the gaoler's presence. He had heard disturbing tales about the girl. When she had arrived in Edinburgh from Glasgow such was her notoriety that vast crowds of people came out to meet her. As she was surrounded, she had called out to a friend of his, a respected goldsmith whose business was in decline, that the falling off in his profits was due to witchcraft. She claimed an image had been made against him. She advised him to look in the corners of his shop. In subsequently doing so, he found a rude little image, made of wax. His assistant Will, on whom suspicion had fallen, protested that Janet Douglas had visited the shop earlier that morning. Whether he was trying to save his own neck they could not be sure. Two of Scott's congregation had also been in the crowd, a devoted couple, married for twenty five years. Janet, ignoring their protestations, accused them of living lately in great discord. She assured them that this change in their relationship was due to an image having being made against them. She pointed at several people in the crowd, accusing them of witchcraft, causing panic and unrest amongst those present. The magistrates, on hearing this, had her immediately arrested and put in close confinement.

Hickes cleared his aching throat and approached the girl. 'Your name is Janet Douglas?'

She looked at him warily. 'You know that it is. Why else would I be summoned here?'

'You need not be suspicious of me. I mean you no harm,' he said smoothly. 'I merely wish to ask you some questions regarding your gift of foretelling the future.'

'So you say,' she retorted, with a cool defiance.

'You doubt me?'

'Words are easy,' she answered, undaunted.

'How can I assure you that my interest is purely academic?'

'By deeds, not words.'

'What do you require of me?'

'A promise, witnessed by these two gentlemen,' she nodded towards Scott and the gaoler, who was gazing, open mouthed, at her brazen cheek. By the cut of their clothes and their Anglicised tongue, the gaoler could see that the two clerics were gentlemen of some refinement. Janet was not in the least over-awed. She treated them as equals. It had been rumoured in the prison that she was a person of quality, from a high born family. Her accent and command of the English language suggested that this was entirely possible.

'What promise do you wish me to make?' asked Hickes curiously.

'That if I answer your questions freely, you will intercede on my behalf with the Privy Council.'

'To what effect?' asked the Reverend Scott.

She ignored him and focussed her unflinching gaze on Hickes.

'That you will use your influence with the Lord High Commissioner to obtain my liberty, on condition that I go to England, never to appear again in Scotland.'

'I cannot guarantee your freedom.'

'But if I can convince you that I have no truck with witchcraft, you can, in turn, do your best to convince your influential friends.'

'I can indeed.'

'You solemnly promise.'

'I do.'

He began to wonder who was on trial here. Her attitude, coupled with the fragile state of his health at that moment, made him want to tell her to mind her place, but he hid his irritation under a mask of politeness.

'Then you may proceed,' she said.

He suppressed the urge to slap her. This was no fourteen year old child as he had been led to believe. Her assurance was that of an older woman.

'You lived in the Highlands before you moved to Glasgow. Is that correct?'

'I have lived in many places.'

'You are a vagabond?' interjected Scott.

She turned a frosty glance toward the tall, gaunt cleric. 'More a curious traveller.'

'Please answer my question,' Hickes continued, slightly aggrieved at Scott's interruption.

'I lived in various parts of the Highlands for a period, yes.'

'And while in Braemar you foretold the bewitching of Sir George Maxwell of Pollok, one year before the event.'

'If you say so.'

'I do not say so, but that honourable gentleman, the Archbishop of St Andrews, has informed me of your claim. He was in the area at the time.'

'Well then it must be true. A man of God would not lie about these things.'

'You believe in God?'

'Of course, sir.'

'Then you will understand,' said the Reverend Hickes 'that lying, deception and the base act of pretending to false revelations are odious in the sight of God.'

She said nothing but looked back at him with an enigmatic gaze.

'You remain silent?' Scott interjected once again.

'I did not realise that was a question.'

'We are not playing games!' said Hickes sharply. 'The consequences of such practices are very serious indeed, injurious to man and offensive to God.'

Again she was silent. He pressed her further.

'I require you, in the presence of God and before two witnesses, to tell me nothing but the truth. Are you agreed?'

'Of course sir,' she said seriously. 'I will tell you nothing but the absolute truth.'

'Very well, then, let us proceed.'

The Reverend Scott leant forward, anxious not to miss

any of her replies. With her oath of truth, Janet's voice had sunk a little lower.

'Do you have the Second Sight? Insofar as you know the things you have discovered?'

'I do.'

'Do you think this gift of Second Sight proceeds from a good or evil cause?'

She hesitated for a moment. 'What do you think of it?'

'I fear it is from an evil cause,' he said plainly.

'I hope it is from good, sir' she replied quickly.

'Does this gift come upon you through any act of your own?' Hickes persisted.

She was silent. Was her silence an admission, he wondered, or perhaps she had not understood the question. 'By which I mean that, prior to these revelations, do you say any words, or perform any actions or ceremonies?'

'No.' Her voice was firm, her look wary. 'Are you sent here to betray me? To accuse me of witchcraft?'

'Certainly not,' Hickes assured her. 'I *am* here to find out the truth of the matter, nothing else.'

It was the Reverend Scott's turn to speak up.

'Do you remember your baptismal vow, Janet?'

'I am unsure of your meaning, sir. I would have been a babe in arms.'

'But your godparents would vow on your behalf. Do you know what that vow entails?'

'Oh, of course sir,' she said quickly. 'I remember now. To renounce the devil and all his works.'

The Reverend Scott exchanged a look with Hickes who took up the role of inquisitor once again.

'Do you understand that by the Devil, we mean Satan, the Prince of Devils and all evil spirits under him?'

'Of course.'

'Do you renounce them all?'

'I do,' she said quietly but firmly.

'Are you willing to renew your baptismal vows at this moment, renouncing once again Satan and all his works and pomps?'

'I am.'

'Then repeat after me . . . '

Janet sank to her knees and repeated the words which the Reverend Hickes had devised. Her expression was a serious one and her tone emphatic. When she had finished, he laid a hand upon her head.

'Janet, do you ever pray to God to deliver you from the power of the devil and all evil spirits?'

She kept her head bowed but said nothing. Reverend Scott looked over at him, with a raised eyebrow.

Hickes put a hand under her chin and raised her face towards him.

'Would you make such a prayer to God, now with me?'

Again, in a firm voice, she repeated the prayer he had composed. He put his hand under her elbow and raised her to a standing position.

'Just a few more questions, if you will bear with us.'

At this point, his throat ached so much that he could

barely speak. He intimated to the gaoler to pass him a jug of the ale lying on the desk, from which he took a sip. The liquid seemed to burn a hole in the lining of his throat on its passage into his stomach.

'Perhaps you have questions you wish to put, Mr Scott?' he croaked.

The latter rose with alacrity and came towards Janet.

She looked at him steadily. He was very aware of her composure and assurance. She seemed untroubled by the line of questioning, now that Hickes had assured her he wasn't trying to trap her.

'Following the execution of the witches of Pollok, you found another case of 'bewitching'?' He said the word with a certain amount of scepticism in his voice, which Janet was quick to detect.

'To which do you refer?' she asked with the same enigmatic expression as before.

'Oh, I forget myself. Of course you have been instrumental in the detection of a number of cases,' Scott said, with a hint of sarcasm. 'This one was in the same month as the unfortunates of Pollok perished in the flames, lit as it were, by your taper.'

She stared back at him, unflinching.

'I know of this particular case,' he continued 'because the reverend gentleman involved, Mr Hugh Smith, Minister of Eastwood in Renfrewshire, is a friend of mine.'

'I did help the reverend gentleman to regain his health.'

'Indeed, he told me in a letter, something of your

involvement,' he adopted an almost theatrical tone as he continued 'how he was brought very low, much afflicted with pain and sweating to the changing of half a dozen shirts some days, but after your 'discovery' of an effigy and the pins taken out, he grew well again.'

He paused and gave her a searching look. 'My question is, how did you know of the existence of that effigy?'

'I know many things,' she replied smoothly.

'So it would seem,' he said, pointedly.

Hickes could imagine the Reverend Scott in his pulpit holding the congregation enthralled. There was something of the actor in the fellow. His heavy-lidded eyes gave him a guarded look; the gateways to his soul almost impenetrable, unfortunate in one of his vocation.

Scott turned theatrically towards Janet, his tall figure almost swooping down on her. 'I repeat, by what means did you know about the existence of that effigy?'

'It was revealed to me while I was in bed . . . by a vision.'

'Was there a familiar involved?' Hickes interjected.

'No, sir.'

'And in the case of Sir George Maxwell,' Scott continued, anxious to press his point home, 'although you had no knowledge of the gentleman at the time, you had a similar vision.'

'Yes, sir. An impression on my spirit which I knew would eventually lead me to Pollok.'

'This was when you were living in the Highlands?'

She nodded.

'And what of your family?' he asked. 'What did they make of these visions?'

'I have no family.'

'Everyone has a family,' he said impatiently. 'A mother and father, at least. What of them?'

She shrugged, but said nothing.

'You have the appearance of a poor girl, who seems, despite your definition of it, to lead the life of a vagrant, yet your words and expressions are those of a better sort. How do you explain this?'

She smiled, a mocking smile. 'Why should you presume that it is so difficult for me to express myself well?'

He ignored her question, disturbed by her assurance, which he was determined to undermine.

'One month after your release from the Canongate prison last year your 'powers of detection' were at work again. Your allegations declaring that Hamilton of Barns was killed by a waxen image, caused another five women, this time in Dumbarton, to be burned at the stake.'

'The image was found. I merely pointed to its whereabouts.'

'And again, only a few weeks later, when the two sons of Douglas of Barloch were drowned crossing a river, during a period when the river was so swollen it should not have been forded, you managed to persuade the grieving father that the calamity was a work of witchcraft. Four people are currently in Stirling gaol as a result.'

'I can only tell what I see in my visions.'

'I am surprised that you manage any sleep at all as troubled as your dreams would appear to be,' Scott said, with heavy sarcasm.

'These are not dreams. Am I right?' Hickes interjected. 'You are awake?'

She nodded.

'I ask this,' Hickes continued 'to ensure whether your Second Sight is by outward representation, by that I mean apparition, or by inward representation, on the theatre of the imagination, caused by some spirit.'

'There are no spirits involved.'

'You are sure of that?' Scott interrupted.

'I have already given my answer,' she said dismissively.

'To clarify,' Hickes continued, aware of Scott's ruffled feathers, but keen to have a final say, 'at what distance do you see persons and objects by means of Second Sight?'

'The same distance they are really from me, more or less.'

'Do you have any trouble, disorder, or consternation of mind, before or after the Second Sight comes upon you?'

'No.'

'Your visions never leave any weariness or faintness upon you?' he persisted.

'Never. I am the same as before.'

'Would you wish to have the Second Sight taken from you, seeing as it has led to your present incarceration?' asked Scott.

'Whatever God wishes,' she replied.

Scott looked at her intently, trying to determine whether she was being sincere. She returned his gaze with a faint smile.

'You may return her to her cell,' said Hickes. The gaoler walked towards her indicating the door. Janet walked through it composedly, without a backward glance.

Chapter Twenty-Four

The Trial of Janet Douglas

Margaret Maxwell listened intently to the evidence in a packed courtroom. She had persuaded her brother, John, to take her with him to Edinburgh when she heard that the trial of Janet Douglas was about to be concluded. The trial, commissioned by the Privy Council, had commenced on the eleventh of March 1679 and had been running for nineteen days. The charge against Douglas was of having a familiar and of consulting evil spirits, but there were no specific demonic details. There seemed to be insufficient evidence for a charge of witchcraft to be laid against her. Witnesses seemed only to confuse with their conflicting testimonies.

Margaret craned forward to hear the concluding evidence of the Reverend Mr Scott, Minister of the Church of the Abbey of Holyrood, who recounted his visit, accompanied by the Reverend George Hickes, to the prison at Canongate, where they had interviewed the accused. In his opinion, he said, based on her answers, she was a cunning impostrix, guilty of a motiveless malignity, obsessed with witchcraft, delighted with the power she had been allowed to exercise over the life and death of her victims.

There was an excited ripple through the court as he stepped down. Margaret thought of the executed villagers of Polloktoun and wondered again whether they had been innocent victims of Janet's obsession. Troubled by these thoughts, she said a silent prayer for the repose of the souls of Jenny Mathie, her family and neighbours.

The Reverend George Hickes was then called to the witness stand. Although present at the same interview with the accused at Canongate prison, he had, surprisingly, formed a different opinion. As one who had made a particular study of the phenomenon known as Second Sight, he gave a rambling account of elf arrows; one shot at a venerable Irish bishop by an evil spirit, which shook the house where the bishop was residing. When interrupted by the Presiding Judge, who asked the relevance of this information, he stated that the subject of elf arrows was of so near an alliance to that of the Second Sight, or Seers, or Visionists and to Witchcraft, that it had been given authentication by the bishop himself.

'Have you proof that Janet Douglas shot elf arrows at anyone?' the Lord Advocate, Sir George Mackenzie, asked impatiently.

'No, M'Lord, but I do feel that the answers she gave to my questions during our interview at the Canongate prison, suggested to me, based on my study of the subject, that she, too, has the Second Sight.'

'You disagree with your clerical colleague, Mr Scott, that this was mere trickery and deception on her part?'

'With respect, I do. I cannot think of any logical reason how she could have such detailed private information about others, prior to their meeting, in the cases which have been mentioned by the previous witnesses.'

'Do you have any doubts, whatsoever, or do you find that her manifestations of the Second Sight match previous cases which you have come across in your learned study of the subject?'

Hickes hesitated. 'Her answers to two of my questions, I confess, do not agree with the usual manifestations of the Second Sight.'

'Would you inform the court where these answers differ?'

'I asked if the Second Sight left any weariness or faintness upon her, or listlessness to speak, walk, or do any other business, to which she always answered no, adding that she was always the same as before.'

'And how does this differ from the cases you have studied?'

'Those possessed of this gift, or burden, depending on

how you consider it, normally complain of a great perturbation of mind,' said Hickes.

'I see. How do you account for this difference in the case of Janet Douglas?'

'In my opinion, there may be a difference in the temperament of those with this ability. Janet Douglas has a bold undaunted spirit and might bear those sights without any fear or perturbation, which others, of more passive natures and less stock of animal spirit, could not endure.'

'Are there other documented cases of those who have borne these visions with equanimity?'

'Indeed, there seems to have been these differences among the prophets themselves. Some, we read, received the prophetical influx with great terror, labour and consternation, of which they complained when their visions were over. They, in fact, desired of God to be excused from the burden of it. While others, we read in the Bible, had no such complaints. It appears to be a question solely of temperament.'

'Am I right then in concluding that, based on your studies in this area, you consider Janet Douglas to be genuine in her predictions?' Mackenzie asked.

'I do, M'Lord. I agree that she, indeed, has wit and cunning, but I am of the opinion that she really is what others think she pretends to be; being induced to that opinion from the notoriety of the facts which the most incredulous and suspicious amongst us cannot deny.'

'Thank you Mr Hickes. You may step down.'

Margaret glanced over curiously at Janet Douglas. The

girl sat unperturbed by all that she was hearing. It was as if the deeds beings discussed were with regard to some other person and had no bearing upon herself. Margaret was confused by the two conflicting testimonies. She was suddenly aware of an undercurrent in the court as Archbishop James Sharp was called to the stand. The crowd was not brave enough to boo his Grace, but people muttered under their breaths. Presbyterian Scotland regarded James Sharp as a Judas. When, as the humble Presbyterian minister of Crail kirk, he was sent to London to remind the restored King, Charles the Second, of his obligation to impose Presbyterianism, and had returned as Archbishop of St Andrews, all regarded him as a turncoat.

The crowd waited in anticipation as he mentioned the various notorious cases of witchcraft with which Janet Douglas was involved. Margaret's brother squeezed her hand comfortingly when their father's name was mentioned yet again. Friends, who had experienced death in their families, warned Margaret that it could sometimes be a year after the event before the worst elements of grief might take their hold. She now appreciated what exactly they had been trying to tell her. At the time of her father's death she had been so focussed on supplying her mother with comfort and strength that her own grief had almost been set aside. Now memories of him filled her with such a sense of loss that she found herself crying at the most inappropriate moments. A hymn, which had been his favourite, sung at the kirk the previous Sunday almost sixteen months after his death, caused her to choke back tears. Finding a necklace in the bottom of her drawer which he had bought for her in Edinburgh, a simple amber pendant, whose existence she had almost forgotten, evoked such painful memories. She had not really liked the piece of jewellery. She was only fourteen at the time, going through a phase when, on reflection, nothing pleased her. She would never forget the look on her father's face when he asked if she liked it. She had merely shrugged, causing a cloud to pass over his eager smiling face. It was painful for her to hear the, by now, familiar details of her father's case and Janet Douglas's part in it. Would her father ever be allowed to rest?

The Archbishop cleared his throat dramatically. 'It seems apparent,' he said, 'as a man of God, that despite those who say we have insufficient proof, I am convinced, bearing in mind the number of witchcraft cases with which Janet Douglas has been directly involved, that she, herself, is guilty of sorcery and witchcraft. Why else would she have this obsession with seeing a satanic presence in other people? There seems no other logical explanation. As the burden of proof be upon us and not considered a proven verdict at this juncture, I strongly advise that, should the accused escape the flames, then she should be packed off to the King's Plantations in the West Indies.'

Janet Douglas jumped to her feet. 'I have a question I wish to put.' Without waiting to see if the Court allowed her to speak, she carried on 'My Lord,' she addressed the Archbishop, giving him an angry look, 'who was with you in your closet on Saturday night last, betwixt twelve and one o'clock?'

The Councillors pricked up their ears in anticipation of a piquant piece of juicy scandal. The Archbishop turned several shades of purple. 'I have no idea what she is talking about,' he stuttered.

'Then let me remind Your Grace,' said Janet. It was her turn to pause dramatically. 'It was the muckle black devil.'

The Archbishop's face relaxed. He smiled at the Court. 'Need I say more?' he asked.

Chapter Twenty-Five

Transportation

James Meikle stood chained to a large burly man on Leith Docks. They were amidst a very mixed group of passengers, the detritus of humanity according to Edinburgh's city fathers, exporting beggars, vagabonds and others *not fitt to stay in the kingdome*. James had been brought straight from the Canongate on a cart, one of many, laden with fellow inmates. It was good to breathe fresh air after the stench of imperfect drainage which pervaded the prison, although his limbs were freezing. Despite the cold breeze, they were being forcibly made to strip off and scrub down. The Captain, Gilbert Gordon of Voyager of Leith, had seen the effects of gaol fever and had no wish to bring contagion on board. James averted his eyes from the shivering women, poor pale wretches, exposed to the elements. A few of them seemed to have no sense of decorum, making little attempt to hide their modesty, all too aware of the leers of the sailors, while others looked as if they wanted to make themselves invisible, clutching their pathetic rags around them as they washed. James dried himself and tried to calm the feeling of panic rising within him. To be banished for seven years, never to see his family during that time, filled him with total despair. He had no idea what Virginia would be like. He had heard the usual tales of marauding Indians and unscrupulous slave-masters. He hoped the reports had been exaggerated.

He caught sight of Janet Douglas standing on her own, a little way off. From the bag at her side she was obviously waiting to board. He was surprised to see his former cell-mate again. She had been, mysteriously, released after her trial. Rumours abounded that it was because she was the daughter of some person of quality who wished matters hushed up. Some spoke of her being connected to Janet Douglas, Lady Glamis, burnt at the stake for witchcraft over a hundred years earlier, or Janet Douglas, illegitimate daughter of the Duke of Hamilton. Could she be part of those families? No answers seemed to be forthcoming. Unknown to James, she had been released on condition that she leave the kingdom within fifteen days. She had been given the luxury of time to sort out her affairs, gather changes of clothes and bathe in the privacy of her own lodgings. James was surprised that she had not run away from Scotland. Of course, if she had been caught she would have been executed. Transportation would seem a happier alternative.

Janet was a little confused on hearing that she was going to Virginia. She expected the authorities to do as the Archbishop had suggested, to deport her to the West Indies. If she but knew, it was not for lack of trying on their part. Her reputation had gone before her. The ships' captains all refused to take her on board. The journey was hazardous enough without someone with a reputation for witchcraft onboard. Captain Gordon had no such fears. He was sceptical about the whole idea of sorcery. Instead, he thought of the money she would fetch, young, not bad looking, in good health and obviously well educated.

Janet stood on the quay, gazing up at the tall masts of the Voyager of Leith as she lay at anchor in the harbour. The ship was a hive of activity. Sailors were busily heaving ropes, others climbing the rigging. Boxes and crates were being carried aboard and stowed below. She was suddenly seized by a harassed gaoler. He gripped her by the elbow and almost force marched her towards the group of female convicts huddled together on the wharf. Once there, he relieved her of her bag and handed it to a sailor who was already carrying the poor little bundles handed to him by her fellow prisoners. Janet ignored the attempts at conversation from the tall wiry woman to whom she was then shackled.

Instead, she watched the progress of the man with her bag, following him with her eyes until he disappeared onboard.

She was suddenly aware that she, herself, was being watched. James Meikle was gazing at her with interest. She remembered the fair haired youth and his fruitless attempts to draw her out while a fellow prisoner in the Canongate cell. He caught her eye and half smiled at her, but she looked away. He wondered what she was feeling, about to leave her native land *for the rest of her natural life,* if the rumours were true. If, indeed, Scotland was her native land. Although she used the odd Scottish word, her accent was not Scots. He had no real idea where she was from, or if there was anyone she would miss. She never talked of family and the only people who visited her while she was in prison seemed to be clerics, intent on finding out her true nature. The anguish of James's leave-taking from his parents, the night before, was still painfully raw. They had made the long journey from Dunfermline to Edinburgh to bring him supplies for the journey and say their goodbyes. His mother had clung to him, sobbing. His father, a man not given to showing emotion, had stood quietly, helplessly, heart-broken, before shaking his son's hand, almost reluctant to let it go. It had taken the reappearance of the gaoler standing impatiently at the heavy door, jangling his keys, before his father released his grip and walked away. They had wanted to come to the docks to see him off, but he had urged them not to. He could not bear to witness their distress.

As James joined the squalid cargo of humanity shuffling up the gangway, leg irons clanking, he thought of his mother and father, God fearing, decent, honest people and wept for the shame he had brought upon them. Wiping his tears hastily on the sleeve of his shirt, he saw Janet ahead of him. She was staring up through masts, spars and rigging to the grey, overcast, sky. There was no sign of distress on her features. He fervently wished he could share her emotional detachment.

Chapter Twenty-Six

At Sea

Four weeks had passed since she last saw sight of land or sea.

The other female prisoners were allowed to go on deck but not Janet Douglas. She was cast in leg irons like the male prisoners. The men were fettered for a good reason. There was always a fear of them rising up, overpowering the sailors and taking over the boat. On Captain Gordon's instructions they were guarded closely. On a previous voyage some prisoners had used a stone to deliberately hole the ship while it was in territorial waters. They then cried out that the ship was sinking, causing the Captain to make for the nearest port. In the ensuing mayhem almost a dozen male prisoners escaped. Now the Captain took no chances. As well as wearing heavy leg irons, they were chained together, severely restricting their movement. The Captain felt that fettering Janet Douglas was unnecessary, but sailors were a notoriously superstitious lot. There was a great deal of unease amongst the crew about her, because of the nature of her crime. Captain Gordon was sceptical about witchcraft, but in order to placate them, he had acceded to their request that she be confined below deck.

Janet was not chained to anyone, unlike her male counterparts, but she was huddled in the corner of a dark hole, a stinking, rolling, grey timbered cavity, secured by leg irons, while the other women enjoyed the freedom of the ship. It was obvious that many fraternised with the crew. They returned below decks with small gifts, including food, which they never offered to share with her. They, too, had heard the rumours about Janet Douglas. They never attempted to even converse with her. She sat there, in her own filth, in a kind of isolation. If it bothered her, she showed no indication of anger or resentment, as the others ate dried fruit, salt beef, or other dainty morsels given by the sailors in exchange for sexual favours, while she had to settle for the meagre ship's rations. She would quietly tap the ships biscuits, removing the weevils before popping the crumbs into her mouth. From what she had overheard in the conversations of her fellow prisoners, the journey to Virginia would take around seven weeks, weather permitting. The other women assumed that because Janet had escaped burning at the stake, she was content just to be alive, albeit in conditions of complete degradation. She appeared to have withdrawn totally into herself. They found her a complete mystery and were happy to keep her at a distance.

Chapter Twenty-Seven

The Storm

The man was bending over her. He had removed his grimy trousers and was fondling himself. Before she could shout out in alarm he had grabbed her roughly and turned her on her face, penetrating her, hurting her with his thrusting, tearing at her young skin. She screamed out in terror, but it wasn't her own screams she heard when she wakened from the dream that haunted her, but those of her fellow passengers. Water was pouring down the hatchways. The hatch covers were gone and the taffrail smashed to pieces by the waves. A gale was blowing hard and the foaming sea was all around them. The women were struggling to keep afloat as their bedding floated by. The water was soon up to Janet's waist. She grabbed hold of a bulkhead and tried desperately to haul herself up, conscious of the searing pain in her ankles as the chains tore at her legs.

In twenty years at sea it was the worst storm that Captain Gordon had ever experienced. The waves were gigantic, huge walls of water unleashing an unstoppable destructive force. They tossed the vessel like a plaything, crashing over the decks, knocking over everything in their path. Two of his most experienced sailors had already been washed overboard. He ran about frantically issuing orders, fearful that the profits from his human cargo were going to be swallowed up by the angry sea. By some miracle, James Meikle managed to keep his head above the water. Others were not so fortunate. Loaded with irons and chained together, they drowned.

For the first time in six weeks James was allowed on deck as the crew manned the bilge pumps in the prisoners' quarters. The storm had retreated, having put up a ferocious fight, leaving the vanquished dead or licking their wounds. He blinked in the strong light and stood shivering, watching quietly as the bodies of many of his fellow convicts were tipped overboard. The prisoner, to whom he was chained, had ingested so much water in his lungs that he died upon the deck. The youth felt little emotion, merely a numbness of spirit, as the big man's body was detached, then thrown unceremoniously into the sea. James's freedom was short-lived. He was pushed forward and chained to another young boy who had lost his partner. About a third of the women had perished too. He looked round in vain for Janet Douglas amongst the survivors, presuming she had drowned, before a sailor suddenly appeared on deck with her. Her clothes were sodden and in tatters. He was surprised to see that she, too, had been in leg irons. Her ankles were encrusted with blood where they had been attached. She met his gaze fleetingly as she was ushered past him and down to the Captain's quarters.

Janet was thrust into a narrow gloomy cabin, lined with dark wood. Although dingy, it seemed luxurious after the confines of between decks.

Captain Gordon wrinkled his nose at the sight of her. She was filthy, streaked with rancid vomit and smelled disgusting.

'First thing we need to do is to get you cleaned up,' he said. 'We'll be in Virginia by the end of the week. Nobody is going to buy you in that state.'

He turned to the sailor. 'Give her soap, water and the best clothes she has in her baggage,' he instructed. 'Oh and some liniment for those cuts on her legs. Then bring her back to me.'

The other prisoners were on deck, already washing and tidying themselves. Janet saw James amongst a group of men shaving off their six weeks growth. Captain Gordon wanted to ensure they looked their best. He was determined that this would still be a lucrative journey, despite his losses. One allowed for human wastage when making these perilous journeys. There was a huge demand for labour. The men with trades would fetch a tidy sum. The others would be hired to work as labourers on the tobacco plantations, if they looked fit enough. He ordered the cook to improve the rations to the prisoners, motivated not by kindness of heart, but profitability. Emaciated prisoners, and there were too many of them, were a liability at this stage. He knew some would join their comrades in the ocean before they reached port but he could always sell the remainder of their rations.

The Captain barely recognised the young woman who now stood before him. Dressed in her best clothes, her hair washed and combed, Janet Douglas could pass for a lady. He dismissed the sailor who had returned her to his cabin and turned to the young girl.

'Sit down, Janet.' He indicated a well-worn chair, looking at her appraisingly, stroking the hairs on his newly clipped beard. She returned his gaze with equanimity.

'I understand that you are conversant with French, Latin and Greek. Is that so?'

'Yes.'

'You have been educated, then.'

She did not answer, merely returning his gaze.

'Answer my question.'

'Apologies. I presumed you were merely stating the obvious.'

Something in her manner really got under his skin. Perhaps because she appeared to treat him as an equal, an inferior almost. She had no sense of place. Captain Gordon felt it was no time for skirting round the subject. He was a plain speaking man and would say what was on his mind.

'If I revealit the charge for which you were imprisonit to potential buyers,' he read from some papers in front of him, *'having ane familiar, consulter with evil spirits,'* he looked up at her 'then no decent person would want you in their household. What say you to that?'

Janet shrugged, seemingly unconcerned.

'You may well shrug, but I dinna think you understand what that means. Let me enlighten you.' He leaned forward. 'Only the most unscrupulous blaggard will take you on. He will use you for his personal gratification. You will be sent out to work the fields from dawn till dusk, workin' wi' the negro slaves in all weathers, beaten by the overseer at regular intervals if you dinna pull your weight. That fine skin o' yours will lose all its youthful bloom. You will no longer be considered a person, merely a commodity to be usit at your master's will. The way I foresee it, you wid be a shrivelled up whore by the time you were twenty.' He leant back in his chair. 'Not a very edifying prospect is it?'

He allowed his words to sink in before continuing.

'Having said that, it is one which many of your fellow prisoners will have to endure, but in their case, for a limited time, seven years or fourteen. In your instance, however, there is no reprieve. Your banishment is for life and what kind o' life would that be? You wid be better tossing yourself ower the side and ending it here and now.'

He looked at her, expecting a reaction, but found it

impossible to judge by her expression what she was thinking. Surely he had got through to her? Fairly safe in that assumption, he played his master card.

'There is, however, a way out. One that would be beneficial to both of us.'

He thought he detected a glimmer of interest in her eyes and carried on.

'I am bound, by law, to reveal your prison sentence and the nature of your crime to a potential employer. I see from your records that you spent some time in the Glasgow Tollbooth for stealing wax from the candle works. Am I right?'

She nodded.

'I will give that as your reason for transportation. The other charges will be oor wee secret.' He smiled. 'Someone with your writing and language skills would be a valuable asset to a gentleman's household. You could hae a comfortable life in Virginia, Janet, if you agree to keep quiet about your so-called witchcraft associations. And I would be paid handsomely for you. So you see, lass, it would be in both of our interests if you do as I tell you.'

He stood up, dismissively. 'Do you agree?'

Janet looked at him steadily, 'I do.'

Captain Gordon gave a half smile, 'Aye, I thocht you wid.'

Chapter Twenty-Eight

Virginia

The air smelled fresh and sweet to Janet after forty-six days incarceration below. She had counted the days as a way of passing the time in the stinking hold, keeping a tally in her head. She had little idea of what to expect at the other end of her voyage. Virginia was only a name to her, although she knew that many merchants in Glasgow were acquiring wealth from the importation of its tobacco crop. She looked over to the far bank, watching a trickle of smoke winding slowly above the trees. The sky was blue and cloudless, the weather warm compared to the cool spring day she'd left behind in Scotland. She heard the gentle swish of paddles as a canoe passed close to the bank, moving swiftly in the opposite direction. Its three occupants appeared half naked, each with painted faces and a single feather in their hair.

'Better mind your hair wi' that lot,' a wiry little sailor muttered in her ear as he passed. Now that they were nearing land he seemed to have lost his fear of Janet. 'They like to attach your scalp tae it!' He gave a coarse laugh as he bent down to pick up a hawser. 'Stand clear! Be landin' soon.'

James looked curiously at the landscape which was to be his new home as the Voyager of Leith sailed into the mouth of Chesapeake Bay. It seemed more like a river than a bay. One of the more talkative sailors, a hard drinking, tough little man known as 'wee Jock,' who looked permanently hung-over, told him it ran into the land for about two hundred miles, 'being everywhere near as wide as it wis at the mouth, aye, and in other places a muckle wider.' James could see a small stockaded settlement of wooden houses up on the hill, a little clapboard church and the fire of a smithy. A small group of men and women watched their approach from the jetty. One woman held the hands of two little girls who jumped up and down excitedly, one pulling on her mother's hand to try and break free. They looked very much like the people he'd left behind. The young man felt a little more optimistic than he had been at any time during the long journey. Perhaps it was because he was now dressed in the new suit of linen clothes which his parents had bought for him.

'If you look like a gentleman,' his mother had said as

she passed the freshly wrapped bundle to him 'they will treat you like one.' Two hours later his mother's words rang hollowly in his ears. He and his fellow prisoners, manacled in pairs, had been marched to a small town, led into a shingle-roofed holding shed where the Captain put them on public display before selling them. James felt like a beast of the field rather than a man. Buyers came up to him, turning him round to examine his limbs to make sure they were sound.

'Let me see him walking,' a tall, powerfully built man, with a pock-marked face, said imperiously. James's chains were loosened and he was made to walk up and down like a horse. His feet and legs were checked. The man forcibly opened the boy's mouth to examine his teeth. 'Our food is hard but homely here. Want to be sure he can chew. Work is hard. He needs to be fit for it,' he said to Captain Gordon.

Before making any decision on James, he moved on to the female prisoners who were standing in line on the other side of the shed from the men. His eye was immediately caught by Janet Douglas who, in her fine linen dress, did not look as if she belonged. Indeed, at first, he thought she was a buyer. It was unusual for womenfolk to carry out slave purchase, but in the case of widows, not unheard of.

He stopped in front of her, sizing her up appraisingly. She returned his look coolly. He felt, oddly, that she was taking his measure. The other women knew their place and dropped their eyes humbly to the ground when he looked at them, but not this one. Whatever she lacked in stature she seemed to have gained in composure and sheer self-possession. He was intrigued.

He crossed over to Captain Gordon who was hovering in the background, occasionally providing a price and background details to potential buyers as they circulated round the shed, weighing up the pros and cons of the human livestock. 'Who is the slight little thing?' he asked, nodding over in the girl's direction. Before the Captain could reply, Janet spoke up in a clear ringing voice.

'Sir, my name is Janet Douglas. What I lack in mere physical strength I more than make up for in educational attainment.'

The man with the pock-marked face rounded on her, amused. 'Do you indeed?' He gave her another appraising look. 'Is this true?' he asked the Captain.

'It certainly is, sir. She is a scholar, reads and writes well, speaks Latin and Greek.'

'And French,' Janet added, composedly.

'By what means did you acquire these?' the man asked. He waited expectantly for an answer, but Janet said nothing.

The Captain hastily drew the man aside. 'What is your name, sir? And if I may ask, what is the nature of your business?'

'Parkins. Edward Parkins. Everyone here knows me. I own one of the largest plantations in the area.'

'Well, sir,' the Captain dropped his voice conspiratorially, 'it is my belief that Janet Douglas is from a noble family, born on the wrong side of the blanket, as it were.'

'Has she given you any indication that this is so?'

'She refuses to be drawn on the subject, but we are both men of the world, Mr Parkins. You know, as well as I do, that many high-born gentlemen sow their wild oats in their youth. Once they are merrit they do not wish reminding o' it. They want the product o' a night of fun, if you'll pardon my indelicacy, removed from their presence, turfed oot, you micht say.'

'I see. What is the nature of her crime?'

The Captain cleared his throat. 'Theft, sir. She stole some wax while working in a candle factory.'

'For what purpose?'

'I am not sure, sir.' Captain Gordon tried to hide his uneasiness. Janet had been accused of stealing it to make waxen images for use against those she accused of witchcraft. How best to equivocate with the truth? Before he could say anything that might be construed as damning, Janet intervened.

'I wanted it to make candles sir, in order to read. My books are my life's blood.'

'Hm. And what is her sentence?' he asked the Captain.

'Banishment for life.'

'That seems a trifle harsh.'

'They wantit to make an example o' her,' the Captain replied hastily. 'Being an educated woman, of coorse. So you see, if you took her on, sir, you would have nae problem of replacement. Naturally, her price would hae to reflect that.'

211

'What are you asking for her?' said Parkins, drawing the Captain discreetly out of earshot of Janet.

The latter saw his face fall. The Captain was obviously demanding an exorbitant fee. Parkins approached Janet again.

'Open your mouth, girl.' She looked as if she was about to refuse but the Captain gave her a warning look. She reluctantly complied.

'Have you children, Mr Parkins?' the Captain asked.

'Three. Two boys and a girl.'

'Are they schoolit?'

'They were. Unfortunately, the schoolteacher succumbed to a fever and died two months ago, along with four of her pupils. 'I have been looking for a governess ever since. I wish them to be schooled at home.'

'Then look no further, sir. You have found one in Janet Douglas,' the Captain said persuasively.

'Mm'. The man was unsure. 'I have been thinking along the lines of an indentured servant. I am wary of trusting my children's care to a convicted felon.'

'But Janet Douglas is no common thief, Mr Parkins. Surely, you can see that, sir?'

Parkins looked hard at Janet, then, without explanation, walked away. The Captain saw the chance of a large profit receding. He knew he was asking a high price for the girl, but was reluctant to budge on it. He watched closely as Parkins walked round to where James was standing. He seemed to be conversing with the boy. He returned a few minutes later.

'I tell you what. Throw that boy in, at three quarters of your asking price for a field worker and I'll take both of them off your hands. Can't say fairer than that. Agreed?'

The Captain thought on it for a moment, then smiled. 'My hand on it, sir.'

Twenty minutes later Janet Douglas and James Meikle found themselves back on board ship. This time it was a sloop which seemed to ply its way up and down the river supplying the plantations with food, equipment and human cargo. They were once again incarcerated in a hold, an even smaller one than before, along with a number of convicts they recognised from the Voyager of Leith. They were crammed together, stifling in the heat while supplies were loaded onboard. Rumours abounded amongst their fellow prisoners. They had all heard snippets of information. They were apparently destined to work on the various tobacco plantations strung out some distance from one another along the region's rivers. There was a great deal of speculation as to what this would involve. Janet took no part in the discussion. She sat in a corner, eyes closed. James envied her ability to fall asleep. His mind was racing, his stomach churning with the uncertainty of what lay ahead. He listened avidly to what everyone had to say, trying to piece together as much information as he could.

Janet was not sleeping. She was merely trying to control the nausea within her. During their brief sojourn on the solid earth of Virginia, the ground appeared to move beneath her. She realised that this was purely due to her experiences of the rolling swell on the Voyager of Leith and her many nights of violent sea-sickness. The river was relatively calm, but the very idea of being back on water made her gorge rise. She did not care what lay ahead of her as long as she could get off this boat. She would meet the challenges ahead of her with equanimity, providing she was on dry land.

Chapter Twenty-Nine

The Plantation

The sun was beating mercilessly down on James's bare head. On arrival at Parkins' plantation the night before, he had been taken to a receiving station and told to strip out of his fine clothes, which were then taken away. 'You'll have no need of finery here,' the Overseer, whip in hand, spat out, grinning malevolently. Instead, James was given a rough canvas shirt and trousers, which irritated his skin, and a kind of hop sack frock. Even his hat, shoes and stockings were taken. Next morning, half blinded by the glare, he stumbled bare–legged amongst the tobacco plants, where he was handed a hoe and told to imitate the actions of the Negro slaves around him. His skin burned and his back ached. He tried to ignore the angry growl of his stomach, for he had been told it would be three hours till food was brought out to them. Is this it? he thought. Seven years of this hell. Never to escape. The Overseer had explained the rules. 'If you run away, when you're recaptured, and make no mistake about it my lad,' he had said, bending over James threateningly, 'you will be; for every hour you're free, you must serve an extra day, for every day a week, for every week a month and every month a year. That's to say nothing of the punishment that's inflicted upon those foolish enough to attempt it.'

He had gripped his whip menacingly. 'So don't even think about it. Of course, if you steal, murder or rob, 'tis a different matter. You're hanged direct.'

Janet Douglas, however, was having a rather different reception.

The Parkins' household appeared to be a comparatively wealthy one. Apart from the large number of field slaves, of whom poor James was one, their large two-storied white house was impressive for the area. Parkins introduced Janet to his wife, Elizabeth, a youngish woman, old before her time, worn down by frequent childbearing. She was currently expecting a child, her sixth in seven years of marriage, one had died in childbirth, another succumbed to fever at the age of three informed the middle-aged housekeeper, Betsy Howard, as she showed Janet around. Betsy initially showed Janet a little deference, impressed by her fine clothes and educated turn of phrase, but on finding out that she was a convict and not an indentured servant, like herself, her attitude changed. Betsy had voluntarily put herself into her position. She was given meat, drink, clothes and lodgings in return for her service of three years, at the end of which she would be free to return home to Bristol. Betsy hoped to marry well and make her life in Virginia, where she knew considerable fortunes could be made. So far, she had been unsuccessful in her dalliances, but with a shortage of marriageable women, even at the age of forty-two, she had not altogether given up hope. She now resented the fact that this convict was to be given the same privileges.

As for Janet, she seemed indifferent to the change in the housekeeper's attitude. Her mistress had suggested, almost apologetically, to her husband, that perhaps Janet should work in the house as a servant, on a trial basis, before entrusting the children to her care. After all, she had said quietly, they knew almost nothing about the girl. Parkins did not like to be questioned in his decisions, but on this occasion, he raised little objection.

Janet had, subsequently, found herself ensconced in the servant's quarters, in this case, a narrow little room on the upper floor, with three beds and a chest of drawers taking up almost all of the space available. Only one of the other beds seemed to be occupied, by a thin plain-looking parlour maid named Annie, just a little older than herself. Later that night, when Janet asked the girl about the empty bed, the parlour maid had been covered in confusion and refused to be drawn. Annie was grateful that her new room-mate did not pursue the matter. Janet Douglas seemed to have a reticence of her own, a reserve, which made conversation difficult. She was obviously exhausted by her long and perilous journey. Before Annie had even blown out the candle, Janet had fallen into a deep sleep.

Chapter Thirty

Compassion

For the next month Janet Douglas kept her head down and attended to the duties of the absentee maid. If she felt that the work of a general dogsbody was beneath her, she gave no indication of resentment. Elizabeth Parkins, her mistress, liked Janet's quiet thorough way of going about her work. If the truth be told, she also liked the plainness of the girl. Perhaps she would not be a temptation to her husband. The buxom charms of Mary, the absentee young servant girl, had proved too much for her spouse to resist. The seventeen year old was currently recovering from the physic administered to her by Parkins on hearing that a bastard child was on the way and he was the father. She had been delivered of a still-born son, but the physic had almost proved as fatal to the mother as to the child. Elizabeth Parkins was as anxious as her husband to cover up events. The Courts took a dim view of masters sexually abusing their servants. Of course Edward Parkins strongly denied having carnal knowledge of the girl, but his wife no longer believed him. There had been too many incidences in the past. Her husband, though a loving father and a good provider, appeared to have some kind of addiction. Frequent sexual activity with her did not appear to satisfy him. When she became pregnant, as she was at the moment, she seemed to disgust him. She asked herself constantly why she stood by him, but sadly came to the conclusion that she had no alternative. She would never leave her children and could not support them on her own. Courts favoured the man in these events. Despite his failings, however, she still loved him and prayed daily that he would change his ways. She made up her mind that she would agree to Janet Douglas being given the governess job and had hinted as much to the girl that morning, subject to her husband's approval. Elizabeth had been sick constantly throughout the six months of her pregnancy and would truly appreciate the children being confined by lessons for a good part of the day. Their boisterous behaviour was more than she could handle in her present delicate condition.

Janet had been busy working in the house, scrubbing and cleaning all morning. She lay back on her bed and looked at her hands in disgust. They had become rough and worn in the few weeks that she had been working in the Parkins household. But, no more, she told herself. Captain Gordon's predictions for her were about to come true. Governess, though still a servant, was of a much higher social standing than housemaid. Her hands would soon recover. Mrs Parkins had given her a few hours off to rest, realising that the girl had been up since five that morning. However, the bright sunny day beckoned and Janet wished to explore her surroundings. She decided to wear the outfit which she'd worn on the day of her arrival and quickly threw off the coarse frock and apron provided by the Parkins. Despite the heat, she donned a pair of gloves to hide her work worn hands and topped her outfit with a wide brimmed hat, edged with pale blue silk. There was no mirror in the room, but she knew, instinctively, that she looked her best. She had not been out of the house since her arrival but, from what she had gathered, Parkins owned a considerable amount of land some little distance from a place named Jamestown, the small settlement they had seen on the ship's arrival.

She walked down the steps and through a rather tired garden, baking in the heat. Mrs Parkins had confessed to her love of flowers, but it looked more of a practical kitchen garden in which a young Negro slave was working. He was repairing a fencing post, no doubt to keep out the hogs and cattle on the other side. He touched his forehead in salute as Janet passed through the open gateway. She looked at him curiously. It was the first time she had seen a black man at close quarters. He smiled, showing a set of even white teeth. She inclined her head in acknowledgment and continued on her way. She had heard from the other servants that Mr Parkins had recently bought twenty black slaves off a Dutch ship. Perhaps this man was one of them? She skirted the house, passing fields of cows and sheep. A brown mare trotted up to the fence post as she approached, flicking its head to shake off the flies crawling into its eyes. She stopped to pat its nose, thinking of the pony she'd ridden, her very own, when she was growing up. She suddenly shook her own head in annoyance. It was no fly which bothered her, but troublesome memories which crept in, unannounced. She refused to dwell on them. That way led to pain and sorrow.

She had only been walking for about ten minutes but was beginning to feel the heat searing through the fine linen of her garments as she approached the tobacco fields. According to the housekeeper, this crop was the source of Parkins' wealth. A cart, harnessed to two oxen, was pulled up at the edge of the field. A thick set white man, his hat set at a jaunty angle, was standing on the cart loading on large greenish leaves, presumably of tobacco, which slaves were handing up to him. She had passed a similar cart on her walk, apparently on its way to one of the tobacco barns. She had seen one of these buildings from the bedroom window. Annie, the parlour maid, had informed her that the tobacco plants were brought there to be air cured.

Rows upon rows of Negro slaves were working busily in the fields. Amongst the black faces she suddenly saw a familiar white one. She barely recognised the young man with whom she had shared a cell in Edinburgh and the nightmarish sea journey which brought them both here. To say that he was white was a contradiction. His skin was burnt a bright red in the fierce unrelenting sun which beat down on his bare blonde head. He looked exhausted, barely able to wield the sharp curved knife with which he was attempting to cut the stalks.

'Is there something I can do for you, Miss?'

She had failed to see the Overseer approach, a look of curiosity on his face at seeing such a fine young lady on his patch. He had been taking his victuals in a nearby shed when he'd spied her from the window and thought he'd better investigate. Perhaps she was carrying a message from Mr Parkins. Janet turned towards him imperiously.

'Why are these men not wearing hats?'

'There's no need, ma'am. These fellows are from Africa, well used to this heat.'

'That one is not.' She pointed to James, who looked on the verge of collapse.

'Pardon me ma'am,' said the Overseer, disliking her tone of implied criticism, 'but who might you be?'

'I am Miss Douglas, governess to the Parkins' household.' Before the man could say anything else, she gazed at him coldly. 'That young man was a prisoner on the ship on which I travelled. I happen to know Mr Parkins paid a goodly sum for him. I do not think he regarded him as a short term investment.'

The Overseer stared at her, confused. 'Not sure I understand your meaning,' he mumbled.

'Unless that young man is given some shade and a cooling drink, he may die from sunstroke.'

As if on cue, James crashed to the ground. There was a commotion amongst the slaves, who crowded round him, concerned.

'You there!' the Overseer pointed to a huge mountain of a man, 'Bring that boy over here.'

The Negro picked up James as if he was a child and carried him over.

'Put him in the shed.'

The man took him inside and laid him down gently on the floor. James slowly came to, and looked around him, confused. Only too aware of Janet at his elbow, the Overseer poured the young man a drink. 'Get that down you.'

James drank the cold liquid gratefully.

'And do not let him back in the fields without a hat,' ordered Janet.

'Don't have a hat for him,' the Overseer said quickly. He had already exchanged the clothes James came with, including his hat, for a fine barrel of ale.

'Yes, you do,' said Janet, taking the hat from the Overseer's head and placing it on James's head. Before the man could protest, she fixed him with a look of sheer malevolence.

'Mr Parkins would hate to hear that the money he has spent on procuring the services of this young man has been wasted,' she said pointedly.

The Overseer fumed, but knew he was defeated.

James tried to mutter his thanks, but Janet had already walked away.

Back in her room, she felt her clothes sticking to her. She had never experienced heat and humidity of this nature. Not even in her time in France. Annie was going about her duties in the house. Janet had the room to herself. She quickly jammed a wedge under the door and undressed, hanging her dress up carefully. She poured some water from the jug on the dresser into a basin, placed a piece of rough cotton material into the water and began to wash the sweat from her body. The cold water felt wonderful on her bare skin. She remembered happy days, as a child, when daily ablutions were of a more luxuriant nature, but again immediately pushed away the memory. She was standing drying her naked body when there was a sudden knock on the door. Before she could call out it was roughly pushed open, the force moving the wedge. She shouted out, but it was too late. The door was pushed again. Edward Parkins was already in the room. She hastily grabbed the piece of cotton towelling against her.

'Did you not hear me call out?' she said angrily.

'You forget yourself,' Parkins said, coldly. 'This is my house. In this place, no doors are closed against me.'

He approached her. Despite himself and the new

resolutions he had made to his wife, he was aroused. He had caught the rounded curve of her young breasts as she turned round. Even now he could see the dark skin of her nipples through the damp cloth which she was pathetically clutching.

'Anyway, I thought you would be anxious to hear the good news.'

His tone had softened. He stood towering over her. She instinctively took a step back.

'Do not be afraid of me, Janet,' he said . 'You will be treated well in my employ. From tomorrow, you are to be governess to my children, giving them daily lessons five days per week. Tomorrow you can spend getting to know them, assessing their needs, judging what books they may need. You will be measured for a new suit of clothes as befits your new status. You will eat with the children of the finest foods. You will be given a room of your own off the nursery.' He looked round the room, before taking a step nearer to her. 'You strike me as the kind of person to whom privacy is important. What say you?' he asked, looking down on her. He found it difficult to read her expression.

'I am most grateful, sir.'

'Well, a little gratitude never goes amiss.' Before she could stop him, his mouth was fastened on hers. One arm encircled her waist while the other tore the cotton towelling from her grasp. She tried to break away but he gripped her arm painfully behind her back with one hand, while the other unbuttoned his trousers. She tried to scream but he quickly placed a hand over her mouth before forcing her onto the bed. She struggled but he slapped her hard across the face, his ring cutting her above the eye. She felt the weight of him on top of her and all the old nightmares returned.

Chapter Thirty-One

Victim

When Annie returned to the servants' quarters some time later, she was surprised to see Janet sitting there, immobile, on the bed, clutching a blanket to hide her nakedness. The parlour maid had never quite taken to the new girl. There was something about her, a distance, an oddness.

'Hey, that is my bed! What's wrong with your own?' she said pointedly.

Janet raised her head slowly. There was a look of real distress in her eyes. It was only then that Annie saw the cut above the girl's left eye, the trickle of blood, the swollen cheek.

'What happened to you?' she said, real concern in her voice, but Janet said nothing. She did not have to. Annie had found young Mary in a similar state after the Master had been in their room. She poured some water from the jug into a basin, soaked a piece of cotton in it, crossed over to Janet and started gently cleaning the area round the girl's eye. When she had cleaned it up, she held the damp cold cloth to Janet's cheek, in an effort to reduce the angry swelling.

'It was him? Wasn't it? The Master.'

Janet remained silent. Annie wondered if she was still in shock.

'Twill be my turn next,' she said. 'I'll kill myself if he touches me.'

She returned to the dresser with the basin.

'Do you want me to bring you up some supper?' she asked gently.

The girl shook her head. She seemed to have lost the power of speech.

Annie took her gently by the arm and raised her up. Janet clung to the blanket like a life-line. It was the first time Annie had detected any sense of vulnerability in the younger girl.

'Why not put on your night-clothes and go to bed? I'll tell Mrs Parkins you are unwell.'

Janet allowed herself to be led over to her own bed. Annie slipped a nightgown over the girl's head and pulled the blanket around her.

'Wish there was something I could do,' she said. 'I told the housekeeper about what he'd done to young Mary, but she seemed to think Mary was askin' for it. Said Mr

Parkins always behaved like a gentleman to her. I reckon he likes them younger,' she mused. 'The girl before Mary was but fifteen when he ruined her.'

She wondered whether Janet was taking in anything she said. The girl had such a strange expression on her face. Shock, she supposed.

'Wonder if it would do any good if I spoke to the Mistress,' she said worriedly. 'Mind you, she knew about Mary, but did nothin'. Still, might make him leave off for a while if his wife knows what he's up to.'

'Say nothing.' Janet had suddenly found her voice.

'Why not?' said Annie. 'I don't want him to come after me.'

'He will not,' said Janet. There was something in her tone, coldness coupled with a certitude that the older girl found disturbing.

'How can you be so sure?'

'He has lain down with Satan and his evil spirits and will perish with them.'

It wasn't just the words which Janet uttered that struck a chill in Annie's heart, but the way the girl said them; with a surety and purpose that she found totally unnerving. She suddenly wanted to distance herself from the room.

'Well, you try and get a good night's sleep,' she said hastily. 'I'll be up later.'

She slipped quietly from the room. Janet closed her eyes. She could not lie on her usual side because of the tenderness in her cheek. Despite that, she drifted into a troubled sleep.

Chapter Thirty-Two

Revenge

Annie had no idea what time it was when she woke up, but it was dark outside. There seemed to be a dreadful commotion going on in the house; terrible cries of pain, like an animal in torment, but human in origin, coupled with children screaming. She sat up as the bedroom door was hurriedly pushed open. Mrs Howard, the housekeeper was standing there, holding a candle. She was in a state of great agitation.

'Annie, Janet, get up! The Mistress needs you.'

Annie rubbed the sleep from her eyes. 'What is it?'

'The Master has taken gravely ill. He's in terrible pain!'

'What is wrong with him?' Annie asked, still half asleep, but swinging her legs out of bed.

'I wish I knew. He is grey as death. Doctor is on his way, but I doubt he'll be in time. Mr Parkins is sinking fast. Hurry girls and come downstairs.'

She left quickly without a backward glance.

Annie dressed hastily and made for the door. She was suddenly aware that Janet had not moved. She turned to the girl, who was sitting up, quite immobile, looking as if she was in a world of her own.

'You best get dressed. Didn't you hear Mrs Howard?'

There was a chilling howl of pain and a calling out for help. Annie recognised it as Mr Parkins' voice.

'Oh, my God!' she whispered. 'He sounds real poorly.'

'Yes,' said Janet, making no attempt to move, but smiling enigmatically.

'He does.'

Epilogue

Chapter Thirty-Three

Hope

On a warm Scottish morning in early summer, Margaret, daughter of the late Sir George Maxwell, was wakened by the child moving in her womb. It was a strange but joyful feeling. She placed a hand gently on her distended belly and felt the limb underneath shift its position. What was it? An arm, leg, a tiny foot? To be inhabited by a growing little person never ceased to fill her with awe. Her happiness, however, was tinged with sadness. Alexander would never see his child. She had been inconsolable after his death. Fallen from his horse, on his way home, he had been found in the river, his skull smashed by a boulder, his mare calmly cropping the grass nearby as the life seeped from her master.

That her young, vigorous husband could be snatched from her, after only a year of marriage, made Margaret rail against God for the injustice of it all. Her fragile faith was almost destroyed. The fact that she might never see him again, however, made her cling to the notion of an afterlife. When she found out, subsequently, that she was carrying Alexander's child she was filled with such joy that something of her faith was restored. As a young girl, she had always declared that, in the unlikely event of her ever marrying, it would not be until she had made her mark on the world, but Alexander had changed all that. A distant cousin from Calderwood, they had not met until seven years after her father's death, but she knew almost immediately that, despite her resistance to the idea of marriage, she did not want to spend her life without this man. Perhaps giving birth to his son was enough of a mark in itself, she told herself. She was certain she was carrying a boy. No matter how irrational her conviction, it was unshakeable.

She worried about the world into which her son would be born. Scotland was a troubled country. Many of its young men had given their lives in its service. She had been visited, the previous day, by her cousin Fergus, who'd lost one arm and part of the other in a ferocious battle at Bothwell Bridge in which the Covenanters had been thoroughly routed by the King's army. Five years on, he was still struggling to come to terms with it. She watched him playing in her garden in the warm sunshine, running around after his little boy, but unable to pick him up. His serious young daughter was gathering petals from the fallen roses, wishing to harness their perfume into one of her own making. She carefully placed them in a container of rain water, which they all had to dutifully inhale and pronounce as fragrant as any of the commercial products which adorned their dressing rooms. The little boy chose this moment to make his bid for freedom, running as fast as his chubby two year old legs could take him. He got as far as the wildflower meadow, at the furthest end of the garden, trampling through the ox-eyed daisies before lying down, exhausted and giggling on a carpet of wild anemones. His father herded him back, with difficulty, using his body to thwart any further attempts at escape. Margaret glimpsed the sadness in his wife's eyes as she watched her husband's struggle. 'At least I have him with me,' she had said quietly. His younger brother, who had managed to emerge physically unscathed from the battle, was still imprisoned for his part in it. He had written to Fergus a few days before, in utter despair. He was about to be transported, never to see friends and family again. 'I wonder, sometimes,' Fergus said to Margaret, with a tinge of bitterness, 'if the Covenanting cause for which we fought and sacrificed was, indeed, the will of God.'

Margaret turned over in the bed and stroked her growing bump. She felt an ache of loneliness. She missed the warmth of her husband beside her, their intimacy, their lively discussions. She found herself talking to the baby, telling him of her hopes of a better world for him to inhabit; a world where peace, justice and tolerance would prevail. When she thought of the terrible events in her own young life, famine, religious strife, the wars between fundamentalist Presbyterians and Episcopalians, the imposition of the death penalty for any Covenanter preaching at a field Conventicle, she despaired. Her own brother, John, had been imprisoned for his Covenanting sympathies. Archbishop James Sharp, who proposed Janet Douglas's banishment abroad, at her trial in Edinburgh, had, that same year, been dragged from his carriage and murdered by extreme Presbyterians. There were those amongst the superstitious, who claimed, however, that all who crossed Janet Douglas met with a tragic end.

Witchcraft trials continued unabated. Society always appeared to need a scapegoat. Despite the Privy Council publicly condemning the use of torture to obtain confessions, it still continued to be practised. Margaret found it difficult to comprehend that a government could subscribe to an ideal, but stand aside and quietly condone when those principles were trampled upon. In the name of power, religion and supremacy, a flawed humanity continued to oppress. Human beings and women in particular, were still being burned at the stake. Despite all this, the flame of optimism still burned within Margaret. She believed in the essential goodness of humanity and trusted that the world her child would eventually inhabit would be a more compassionate and enlightened one.